Dawn of CTHULHU

...and other Curious and Exotic Speculations

By

D. G. Valdron

FOSSIL COVE PRESS

Winnipeg, Manitoba

Fossil Cove Publishing
1301 - 90 Garry Street
Wpg, Man, Canada, R3C 4J4

Cover: Richard Curtecka © 2012. The Sunken Continent of Zealandia, as it would appear above water, twenty million years ago.

Issued in electronic and print formats

ISBN:
978-0-9879061-5-1 (ebook)
978-1-998453-21-4 (IngramSpark trade paperback)

Text set in Garamond

Dawn of Cthulhu - Contents

PART ONE:

On the Worship of Dark and Monstrous Gods

The True History of the Mythos

(Lecture Series, Course 4.22, Fall Semester Senior Lecturer, Pickman Marsh)

Welcome to our class. If you can settle down please. That's it. Thank you.

Now, I suppose most of you are here because you've imbibed the works of lurid 1930's pulp authors - Howard Philip Lovecraft, Clark Ashton Smith, Robert E. Howard, Edgar Rice Burroughs, Robert Bloch, August Derleth and whatnot. Ah, I see the glints of recognition.

And so you've all been steeped in the dark stories of the Cthulhu cult, a mysterious worldwide cult of immense antiquity, predating Christianity, worshiping a multitude of alien gods, with chapters flung around the world, from New England to Malaysia, a sect devoted to secrecy and assassination. All of this is nonsense.

Here is the truth: The Cthulhu cult, as it is called, is simply a worldwide religion of immense antiquity, predating Christianity, devoted to the worship of a pantheon of nonhuman gods, protecting itself through secrecy and assassination, and whose adherents range the world from Greenland to Polynesia.

You see? Two fantasy and reality. Two completely different things.

The difference? Didn't you spot it?

Mystery.

In the first, the Cthulhu Cult is mysterious. It is a mystery. It is a journey into the black fountains of, not just the unknown, but the unknowable. How old is the cult? Ageless! From the very dawn of time! Where does it spring from? The abyss! The ape men worshiped it! Where is it? Everywhere and nowhere! What are its rites? Unspeakable and indescribable!

Poppycock!

Well this is not a mystery, this is history. We acknowledge the unknown and advance upon it. We do not bow to the unknowable and cower before it.

The Cthulhu Cult is not a product of the abyss, but an artifact of history. It is describable, definable. The Cult is knowable.

Stop and think about it? Where does the cult come from? The answers are right there in front of you. Look at them, look at their Gods: Azathoth. Yog-Sothoth. Dagon. Hastur. Nyarlathotep. Shub-Niggurath. Tsathoggua. Ithaqua. Our squid headed friend Cthulu.

Where did these names come from? What language, what culture birthed these names? History is everywhere. Nothing comes out of nowhere. Everything in this world, you see, has a provenance. It has a history, and it wears its history on its face.

So we look at the chief deities of the cult: Azathoth and Yog-Sothoth, and what do we see? We see their past, written plainly upon their present. We see Thoth. Egypt's Thoth.

Dagon and the Three Faces of Thoth

Ah, what is that I spy? Dawning comprehension? Come on, none of you ever noticed? Azathoth - Aza...Thoth. Yog Sothoth - Yog-Sot...Thoth. How about Nyalathotep? Nyarlat... Hotep! Perhaps not. Shall I draw a picture?

Yes, we can find the beginnings of the Cult not in the ageless abyss, but in a very specific and well known time and place. Ancient Egypt.

Oh wait though? What about Dagon? Very much a Phoenician deity! No problem there, we have a little divine pilferage. What about Cthulhu? Shub Niggurath? Hathor? Tsathoggua? Ithaqua? Where do they come from? Definitely not Egyptian, but they each have their secrets to reveal.

But if the Cthulhu cult is simply another Egyptian cult, a spin off of from Egypt's numerous pantheons, then why does it diverge so strongly? And why does it alone survive to this day? What was so special about this cult that it outlived all the polytheists faiths of its day.

The answers are there to find. The history of the cult is written on its face, in its names and traits.

First, if we can establish that the cult's origins are Egypt, that's where most of their gods, and especially where their most important gods, are derived. The presence of other gods, the Phoenician's Dagon, most significantly, tells us that it is not wholly an Egyptian faith, but a hybrid. It may have started in Egypt, but it has mingled with other faiths, it has mutated and evolved.

Let's go back to Egypt for a moment. We've identified the two principle deities as being descendants of Thoth.

Who was Thoth? He was the Ibis headed God, the god of scribes, of numeracy, of literacy. He was the god of trades and merchants. That attribute came with being the god of scribes. A successful merchant lived by his ability to keep accounts and ledgers. He is the arbiter of good and evil. He is the creator of science, of philosophy and magic. He is the author of mathematics, and it was he who set the stars in their courses... making him, by extension, the God of navigation.

Thoth's relative importance in Egypt's pantheon rose and fell, of course, with the fortunes of the various temples. Egypt was a land of many gods, many temples, many regions. At times, Thoth moves to a pivotal point in Egyptian mythology. In other eras he becomes a peripheral figure. In some places, in some trades, he is strong. Elsewhere he is weak.

But notably, he was important enough to the people who founded the Cthulhu Cult. He became not just one, but two gods, and the most central ones to boot. That tells us something. Thoth was not just a lucky god, rather, he was central to the Cult pantheon because his qualities, his aspects were central to the people involved.

Who were these people? Lurid pulp novelists perhaps, like our friend Lovecraft? No? Scribes maybe, accountants, merchants, traders, possibly navigators. That sounds like Thoth's sort of people. But how can we be sure? Perhaps by looking at other evidence?

Perhaps by looking at some of the company our friend Thoth is now keeping?

Dagon! A God of the Phoenicians. The Phoenicians of course were legendary sailors and traders throughout the Mediterranean and beyond.

What's Dagon doing hanging out with Thoth?

Whatever the reason was, Dagon was subordinate. Too much of the Cthulhu pantheon, in one form or another, can be traced back to Egypt. The Egyptians are the dominant influence. The Phoenicians are hired hands, along for the ride, and bringing a god or two along.

But interestingly, Dagon's name doesn't change much. Thoth morphs all over the place, so do the others. Dagon is more pristine. Who was Dagon?

He was a Phoenician and Semitic god, originally associated with grain and agriculture, the god of rains, but also of fishing. This makes him, of course, a very fundamental god - he was the god who was putting bread... or fish... on the table.

Dagon begins in the Mesopotamian region as early as 2500 BC. Dagon's worship peaked around 2300 to 1800 BC, when he was the head of city Pantheons, of many cities: of Ebli, Tuttul, Irim, Ma-Ne, Zarad, Uguash, Siwad, and Sipishu.

However, by 1300 BC he fell to third rank. Thereafter he seems to have been in decline, until by about 500 BC, he was a relatively minor figure. A god, definitely, but not one of the movers and shakers. He's a progenitor god, the father of younger gods who start to take priority.

So how does he sneak into the Thoth-based Pantheon? And how does a god primarily devoted to the plough become a fish god?

Turn those questions on their head: Dagon sneaks into the pantheon. And he becomes a big fish god, which is to say, parts of his nature are emphasized, and parts minimized or abandoned. What does that tell us?

The Phoenicians had hundreds of Gods to choose from. They could have picked any god. Why Dagon? The Carthaginians went with Moloch, after all.

We can assume that the Phoenician's who contributed to the Cthulhu Cult must have picked Dagon because he was the important god to them at the time. If these Phoenicians imported Dagon into the cult, then it stands to reason that it must have been from a place and period when Dagon was still a major god. Which puts the Cult somewhere in the period of Dagon's prominence, between 2300 to maybe 1300 BC. Any later than that, he's not a mover and shaker, he's a has-been god. Some other god would have taken his place.

Another quality of Dagon: He's very much a bread and butter god. Or perhaps bread and fish. Thoth is concerned with all the airy fairy things, like writing things down, balancing scales, doing math and accounting, all very important. But Dagon is a god for when you want to be fed. He is a practical God.

This tells us a little bit about the relationship between the Egyptians and the Phoenicians. The Phoenicians are definitely the hired hands. The big god is Thoth, Egyptian, and all about the big picture - strategy, accounting, abstract stuff. The subordinate God is Dagon, Phoenician, and concerned with the practicalities of the day.

This relationship tells us a little more. Dagon is a big god, so he's allowed in. But he's not the biggest god of the Phoenicians. There can only be one Chief. The Egyptians weren't going to allow the Phoenician's to import a god who was number one. That would be a challenge to Thoth. Nope, he's a subordinate god. Important enough to merit consideration, but not so much as to rock the boat. Which puts the cult at some point during Dagon's decline from top spot, when he's descending, but not yet irrelevant.

Oh, and Dagon evolves to be a fish god. A sea god. That's tells us that his significance shifts towards the sea, that's where he becomes more important - for fishing and sailing. And of course, the Phoenicians are renowned sailors.

Why would the Egyptians accept a foreign God at all? They have plenty of their own. Dagon's inclusion must represent a pragmatic decision. Something important enough to compromise theological purity. The Egyptians need the Phoenicians for something, and need them enough they'll tolerate importing a deity. We did say the Phoenicians are renowned sailors.

So Traders and Scribes need Sailors? The cult is shaping up as an expedition! It's a trading expedition. You don't need a god of accounting if you are going to war. Conquest requires armies not ledgers. And it's a sea expedition, or you wouldn't be hiring Phoenicians, and the Phoenicians wouldn't be praying to the sea-side aspects of their gods.

Our friend Cthulhu, he of the squid-head. Well, there's another sea deity for you. He of the Squid head and dragon.... or is it crocodile body? Definitely a sea deity. Definitely Egyptian influence too. The Egyptians were famous for sticking animal heads, and sometimes animal bodies, on their mix and match gods. A squid? That's a bit out there. But the underlying concept of grafting non-human aspects, stitching animal parts onto their gods, that's very Egyptian.

Of course, there's no Cthulhu or equivalent in Egyptian mythology.

But look across the red sea. Who do we find? The peoples of the Arabian peninsula, the cultures which would evolve into the Nabateans, who would in turn be the ancestors of the Arabs that we know today. For our purposes, we'll simply refer to them as the Nabateans.

Who do these early Nabateans worship? Their own pantheon of course, but I'll mention two of them. The first is Aza or Uzza. This is the chief god of the Nabatean pantheon, a creator and fertility goddess. Aza.... As in Aza-Thoth?

And the other? Kutbay? Who is Kutbay? He's the Nabatean god of scribes, of literacy. He is the Nabatean version of Thoth! So the Cthulhu Cult's three most important Gods: Azathoth, Yog-Sothoth and Kutbay or Cthulhu as he came to be called, are all just Thoth. Three Thoths in one pantheon! I'm sure there's a joke in there.

Our expedition is not just Egyptians and Phoenicians now. There's a third group, the Nabateans. As I've said, technically, they're probably not Nabateans, but the peoples who inhabited the Arabian peninsula, and gave rise to the Nabatean and then the Arabs. But we'll continue to call them Nabateans for the sake of convenience.

These Proto-Nabateans are clearly subordinate to the Egyptians.... most of the Pantheon is still Egyptian derived after all. But they are important. They import more of their gods, and their gods get more respect. One merges with the chief Egyptian god, another takes a high rank. The Nabatean component seems more important than the Phoenician's, but they also dissolve more. Dagon retains more of his identity than Cthulhu, who evolves and changes as he's incorporated.

Dawn of Cthulhu – Page 8

The Nabatean presence, and the importance of the Nabatean presence seems to point us towards the Red Sea. I'll come back to that.

Now, we've seen Egyptian gods, we've seen Nabatean gods, we've seen Phoenician gods.

Whose gods haven't we seen?

Anyone?

That's right: Greeks. No Greek gods in the Pantheon. Or at least none that we can recognize.

What does that tell us? The absence of Greek influence in pantheon suggests that the Cult emerged before the Greek Civilization became a dominant or even a formidable presence. So, before Alexander. Alexander conquered the known world, including Egypt, and saddled the Egyptian's with the Ptolemies. A dynasty which brought Greek culture to Europe. Alexander was about 300 BC.

But even before Alexander, the Greeks were getting around. They were sailing around the Mediterranean. They were getting in fights with the Persian Empire. If we're generous, we can put the era of the Greek explorations and expansions back as far as 800 BC. Which suggests that the Cult's origins take place before 800 BC.

Alternatively, we might speculate that our hypothetical seagoing merchant expedition is taking place so far away from the Greek sphere that not even residual cultural influences occur. There's something to that. The Pre-Nabateans are very important, which seems to put us in the Red sea and away from the Mediterranean, relatively remote from the Greek sphere.

But the Phoenicians are involved, and the Greeks aren't? It's not just the Red sea. We are looking at a historical period when the Phoenicians were the 'go to' sailors, and the Greeks weren't.

So there you have it: The Cthulhu cult begins as a seagoing merchant expedition by the Egyptians, down the Red Sea, using Nabateans and Phoenicians as hired hands, sometime between say 1800 BC and 800 BC.

Can we narrow it down a little further?

We can draw a few more conclusions. First - this had to have been a distant expedition. They weren't close to home. If they were close to home, they would have stuck pretty close to official doctrine. There would have been no mixing and matching of deities, Thoth would have stayed Thoth, and Dagon and Kutbay would have stayed in separate pantheons, thank you very much. The temples and the priests, if they were close enough, would have enforced doctrinal purity.

Whoever these people were, they were far enough from home that a Priest wasn't going to show up at their elbow to scold them whenever they wandered off the theological ranch. They were far enough away that they could start to be flexible with their gods.

Secondly - this had to have been a sustained expedition, one with a long, long period, not just of isolation, but duration. Nobody invents a new religion over their summer vacation. Well, almost nobody. We're talking decades, perhaps generations, maybe even centuries.

We know where they began - Egypt, Lebanon, Arabia. Those are the roots. But where did they emerge? A long long time ago, in a place far far away. At least in ancient terms.

Let's go now, and take another look at Egypt. But this time, we're going to get a little more specific. We're going to zero in a bit on the Egyptian New Kingdom.

The New Kingdom of Nyarlathotep

The New Kingdom endured from about 1550 BC to 1077 BC. During this period, Egypt achieved its maximum territorial expansion. Egyptian campaigns extended the power of the Pharaohs north, through Palestine, Lebanon, Syria even to the coasts of Turkey, where they battled the Hittites inland. Of course, this realm included the Phoenician cities. In the south, the Egyptians pushed down over-running or dominating the kingdoms of Kush and Nubia, extending Egyptian power and influence almost the length of the Red Sea.

This was an age of vast wealth and power. Egypt ruled much of the known world, or at least the world it cared to know. There were the Mycenaeans and Minoans in the north, the Hittites in the northeast, and ne'er do wells all along remote European shores - but none of those counted for much of anything.

But crucially, the New Kingdom had extended its power to the point where it was just short of the horn of Africa and the Indian Ocean - of the exotic lands, the apes and ivory, gold, jewels, plants, spices and aromatics of Africa, the Arabian peninsula and the Persian Gulf. For the first, and perhaps only time in Egyptian history, they were almost within reach of whole new worlds.

And the height of the New Kingdom was the reign of Amenhotep III, 1386 to 1351 BC. A thirty-five year reign of unprecedented power, prosperity, cultural and artistic achievement. Get out your notepads, because Amenhotep III's full name is Nebmaatre Amenhotep III. Ladies and gentlemen, I give you Nyarlat-Hotep. Nyarlat being an obvious contraction and corruption of Nebmaatre.

Now, I want to speak a little bit about Nyalathotep in the theology of the Cthulhu cult. Nyarlathotep is a unique deity. He is the intermediate deity.

Most gods... Most gods are 'over there'... They're up in the sky. They're deep in the ocean. They're not here with us. They're somewhere else, remote and above and beyond. Not the Greek gods of course. They were always getting involved with mortals, often getting into bed even. But by and large, gods are supernatural entities governing the operation of the world, and quite inaccessible to the mortal sphere.

They don't associate with the riff raff. That's what priests are for, to mediate between the humans and the gods.

Mostly, the Cthulhu cult gods follow the familiar pattern. They're impersonal and remote, way out there in heaven or on some mountaintop. Nyarlathotep doesn't follow that pattern. He's a trickster god, he's full of temptations and wonders, he gets involved with people, he brings messages and mediates among the gods.

In some ways he resembles the Greek Hermes. He's the god who is situated at some midpoint between the gods and humanity. He's a god, but he's not like the other gods. He is different.

The theory is that most gods originate through our attempt to put a name and a personality on the impersonal forces of nature. But once in a while, as it happens, a local boy makes good. The theory is that every now and then, some mighty king, some hero, some cultural figure manages to make such a splash that the succeeding generations will eventually elevate them to godhood.

That happened with our friend Hercules, who allegedly started off as a mortal, but got a ticket to Olympus. The Roman emperors and Egyptian pharaohs were big on this idea, but it takes more than pronouncing yourself a god for it to really catch on. Still, the fact remains, that at the right time, the right place, catch the right cultural wave, you might coast all the way up to divinity.

This is Nyalathotep. He's an anomaly god. But he's got all the characteristics of an elevated mortal, someone who was originally just a king, but who time and theological hijinx has morphed into something more. These are the characteristics of the Nebmaatre, the greatest, the most successful, one of the longest reigning pharaoh of the New Kingdom. Nebmaatre, accorded divinity as a pharaoh. Nebmaatre the conqueror.

And Nebmaatre Amenhotep, the pharaoh who commissions, and funds and directs the trading expedition which will evolve into the Cthulhu cult. Thus, a trader, a bargainer, a scribe and accountant, a collector and bringer of wonders, the bridge between humanity and the gods. For this, he is eventually elevated to full divinity, and remembered as Nyarlathotep.

So there it is -we have fixed the Cult's period of origin, through the footprints of its scripture: Somewhere between 1380 and 1350 BC, the Egyptian New Kingdom at its peak, a trading expedition down the Red Sea to the Indian Ocean, to exploit the riches of Asia and Africa.

What did I tell you? Nothing mysterious about it. The cult wears its origins, its history, on its face. All we have to do is look at a few names, and we have the story.

And that's enough for now.

Next time, we'll examine the evolution and history of the cult, its role in the ancient world, and its survival into modern times. Class dismissed.

The Pharaoh's Expedition to Strange Lands

Welcome back, I'm glad to see to many of you survived to return.

We were exploring the Cthulhu Cult, and its origins in a trading mission to the Indian Ocean, commenced at the peak of the Egyptian New Kingdom, by the Pharaoh Nebmaatre Amenhotep, who would eventually become Nyarlathotep, of a mongrel pantheon derived from Egyptian, Phoenician and Nabatean deities, somewhere between 1380 and 1350.

The first question is why? What was it that Nebmaatre wanted?

In fact, there had been trade down the Red Sea, going back as far as 2500 BC, at least to King Khufu of the fourth dynasty. There are records of an expedition commissioned by Pharaoh Sahure of the fifth dynasty. More expeditions followed during the sixth, eleventh and twelfth and eighteenth dynasties.

Most of these were actually expeditions - ie, major, expensive and very occasional projects.

The Egyptians were fine hands at going up and down the Nile. They were not good with open sea sailing, even in the comparatively narrow and sheltered waters of the Red Sea. There was nothing like a steady or regular trade for perhaps a thousand years. It is not until the 18th dynasty that

Hatshepsut builds a fleet to facilitate regular crossings of the Red Sea, although this regular trade died down afterwards.

The principal trade goods were gold, bitumen which was essential to mummification, aromatics like frankincense and myrrh. This is not to be underestimated. Nowadays, incense is simply for bathtub relaxation. In those days, before regular bathing, aromatics had powerful magical and religious significance. Especially in cities full of unwashed bodies and poor sanitation and dubious post mortem practices. Myrrh was literally worth its weight in gold. Copper was a trade good. There was ivory, wild animals and animal skins, birds and exotic feathers, exotic woods like ebony.

Now, a lot of these products had been in Egypt initially. There were North African elephants, and ivory up to the time of Hannibal. Ostriches also roamed as far north as Arabia.

Egypt had been civilized for a long time, and what we saw during their long period of civilization was the steady depletion and extinction of the large fauna. Local deposits of naptha had been mined out over centuries. So the Egyptians had to go further and further afield. As Egyptian fauna were obliterated, other easily accessible North African fauna were steadily wiped out.

Quite quickly, the only place left was the south. Of course, most of these goods of this could be obtained through the river trade, or overland trade. And indeed, there was enough of that over a long enough time, that really, we would only see the occasional Red Sea expedition.

There might be big money in a sea expedition south, but it was also a massively expensive and difficult project for the Egyptians, and there were constant interruptions, crises, dynastic battles, civil wars, rise and falls. It was difficult to build a sustained impetus.

But over a time span of 1200 years, several things are happening. The Egyptians are having to trade further and further overland for the things they want and need, and it is getting more and more expensive and difficult.

But as the Egyptians travel further south along the Red Sea, they encounter more and more potential trade goods. They trade into new regions, encounter items that they've never heard of, like black wood, and they take it home. There's a demand, there are new demands. The remote regions of their trading network start to overlap with the fringes of other trading networks in the Persian Gulf and Africa.

Finally, the Egyptians are also getting steadily better at sailing. Well, not really. But they're getting to know the Phoenicians, who are good at sailing, and they're becoming wealthy and willing enough to hire them. By the time of Hatshepsut, the relationship with the Phoenician sailors is almost a regular thing.

This is what we have when we come to the New Kingdom and Nebmaatre Amenhotep. We have an Egypt at the absolute height of its wealth and power. We have an elite and royal class which has money to spend, and we have overland trading networks and an increasing number and frequency of sea expeditions which are bringing an increasing assortment of valuable goods in.

So Nebmaatre Amenhotep decides to do something that the Egyptians have never done before. The earlier fleets are simply one time expeditions. They go out.... and they all come back.

But this time is different. Nebmaatre doesn't just send a fleet. He doesn't even just send a large fleet – He sends a literal armada and by all accounts, it was immense. Nebmaatre commissioned something like ten times as many ships as Hatshepsut. He sends them out to stay. Their mission is to found and anchor permanent trading posts.

This is without precedent in Egyptian history. The Egyptians conquered, yes. But this isn't conquest. Nebmaatre is not sending armies. He's sending embassies to support his trade. He wants regular, stable transmission and traffic of goods back to Egypt.

Why is he doing this? The problem with single expeditions, go out, and come home, is that you have to rebuild your infrastructure every time you do it. You start from scratch, you have to build the ships, hire the crews, go exploring, make contacts. It might be worth it, but it's a huge investment, and even if the returns are colossal, it's not the sort of venture that's easy to do again and again.

But Nebmaatre is thinking that if he sets up a permanent or long term trading network, then he can avoid the duplication of effort, the starting from scratch investment and development costs of single expeditions, and he can achieve a much larger volume of trade and trade goods. In the long run, it will make a lot more economic sense, and be much more profitable.

A long term project like that is immensely more expensive than a single modest expedition. But the Egyptian New Kingdom is at the height of its wealth and power. Amenhotep Nebmaatre is a Pharaoh who thinks big.

Of course, he's not sending his expeditions into the desert or the jungle. Rather, this is the land of Punt. There are already cities and kingdoms there. Places like Mosylon, Opone, Malao, Avalites, Essina and Tabae on the Somali coast, Saba and Hadramaut on the Arabian coast.

This makes things simpler. After all, creating an entirely self sufficient colony is immensely expensive. You can't just put a bunch of traders down. You have to ensure they're fed, which means you need farmers, who need land and beasts of burden. The farmers need tools, so you need artisans and trades to support the farmers and make their tools. And of course, you need soldiers to defend the traders and artisans and farmers and their lands and animals. If that's all waiting for you ready made its much easier. But that also means you are at the mercy of the local population and their rulers, which requires a certain diplomacy, and means a certain vulnerability. The Egyptian army is a long way off.

But it worked. The first trading post was at Opone. A second at Saba. And then Essina. At some point, local opposition perhaps, the post at Opone was closed and moved to Mosylon. It was re-opened a decade later as the Egyptians learned to play the locals off against each other.

For decades, the trading posts multiplied and grew, sending a steady stream of exotic goods back to Imperial Egypt.

Then, disaster struck...

His name was Akhnaton.

The Black Pharaoh and the Nameless City

With the passing of Nebmaatre Amenhotep III, came the ascendancy of Amenhotep IV, who we know of as Akhnaton.

Akhnaton, who ruled Egypt for seventeen years, is somewhat of a famous figure in Egyptology for three reasons - his wife Nefertiti, whose unearthly beauty is preserved in the famous bust. His son, Tutankamen, who we all know as King Tut and the discovery of his tomb, and of course for Akhnaton's own early experiment with monotheism. As monotheists ourselves we like to think of Akhnaton as enlightened, progressive and ahead of his time.

That's not how the Egyptians saw it, unfortunately.

Upon taking the throne, Akhnaton began an expensive new program of public works. But this wasn't enough. He decided that he needed a new royal city, Akhetitan, built on a marshy shore of the Nile. It was a difficult, unpleasant and ruinously expensive monument to his own ego.

While that went on, Egypt went to pot. The people of the Nile experienced the first of several pandemics or plagues. The expenses of the massive construction program for Akhetitan - new capital cities don't come cheap - drew money away from other sectors of society.

The Empire started to go to pieces. We have correspondence from far flung provinces begging for support and money against the Hittites. The temples became restive as they saw their revenues siphoned away.

In response, Akhnaton centralized the religion, all but overthrowing the normal flow of Egyptian society. For Egypt, Akhnaton was a nightmare, bringing disaster, ruin and chaos everywhere.

For Nebmaatre's far flung trading posts, initially, all was well. They were insulated from most of the political and social shocks of Akhnaton's reign, at least for the first decade.

But as Akhnaton tightened his grip, and as Egypt's finances worsened, the trading posts were abandoned. Simply abandoned. Akhnaton just decided to forget about them. The trading posts were a minor provincial project of his father. He concerned himself with more important things, like rebuilding Egypt in his own image.

There was likely some effort to return home by many of the traders. But the Egypt they were coming back to wasn't the place they'd left. It was a place of plagues, of turmoil, of religious repression, of bitter politics. There was simply nothing to return to.

Some trade back with Egypt continued, but as much as 90% simply withered. The trading posts, the settlements survived by supplementing the reduced Egyptian trade with increased local trading, playing their hosts off against each other, and by offering what their hosts lacked - better boats. The Phoenician sailors were forced to travel further along the African and Arabian coasts, using their superior seamanship and seacraft to eke out a living.

Akhnaton died of course, and after perhaps a decade, Egyptian society slowly righted itself and went back to the old ways. Akhnaton's political enemies, the temples, re-emerged, and they proceeded to wipe out his legacy.

Actually, there was a concerted effort to write Akhnaton out of history entirely. His name was chiseled off inscriptions, he was struck from the records and official histories. His city was abandoned to the marshes, and soon, all that the Egyptians remembered of his period was a continuous disaster.

The trading posts resumed regular contact with Egypt once again. Prosperity returned.

But the expatriate Egyptians of the trading mission remembered Akhnaton. If Nebmaatre Amenhotep would be worshipped and be elevated to godhood as Nyarlathotep, Akhnaton would be recalled as the author of evil and disasters.

He entered the cult lore as the 'Black Pharaoh', and his City, Akhetitan went into their records as the 'Nameless City' abode of crocodiles. Which is where Mr. Lovecraft and his friends picked it up. In their way, the Cult was simply following the tradition of the day in trying to purge Akhnaton from history and memory.

The Akhnaton era had two major effects on the emerging Cthulhu cult. The first was the break with Egypt. Under Nebmaatre Amenhotep, the trading posts were essentially a royal project, and we find ample correspondence demonstrating that the strings were quite tight. Akhnaton cut them loose, and although trade with Egypt resumed after him, the trading posts were no longer a venture of the Pharaohs, but were basically independent.

The other effect was a very early and very determined inoculation against Monotheism. Separated by distance, the Egyptians of the trading posts had a very good window into Akhnaton's efforts to impose monotheism, and had not liked it at all. They'd bowed when they had to, lied where they could, and argued it out privately. The ability to co-exist with and resist in the face of powerful monotheist influences would become a signature of the Cults later success.

Together, these two events produced a very critical result - doctrinal separation. Much like Henry the Eighth used a combination of politics and geography to separate from the Catholic Church, the early trading posts less willingly, had been cast adrift. Their faiths were no longer derived from the doctrines of the Temples in Egypt.

Rather, from Akhnaton onwards, the trading posts would describe and define their own doctrine, and like the Church of England, would descend into a twisted abomination of perversion and licentiousness.

Haha. Just kidding.

Not about the Church of England of course, they really are a cavalcade of perversions and abominations.

Class dismissed, when we return, we will cover the Post-Akhnaton era of the New Kingdom.

Azathoth, Yog-Sothoth and Cthulhu

Welcome back. All still alive I see? Well, most of you.

Let us return to these ancient Proto-Cultists, and the examination of the Akhnaton Schism, which is so pivotal to the emergence of the modern cult.

Now, there were different ways this could have all turned out. Egypt could have retained or recovered direct control and supervision of its trading posts, and perhaps over time, this might have lead Egypt to a new kind of imperialism and a thalocrassy or 'sea-empire' around the western Indian ocean. But instead the trading posts had been cast adrift, becoming an independent entity.

The trading posts could have simply been absorbed into the local population, vanishing from history, with the exception of perhaps a few interesting ruins, and cultural survivals. That could have happened easily.

In fact, there's some evidence that it did happen here and there in some areas and to some limited extent. If Akhnaton's policies had continued for a few more decades, that's exactly what would have happened - where else did the trading posts have to go? What other options did they have left? They could go home or they could join with the locals.

The Akhnaton schism turned out to be a passing thing. It lasted just long enough, less than twenty years, for the network of trading posts to become irrevocably independent and autonomous. But not so long that their fates were sealed and they were doomed to be absorbed by the locals.

Instead, after a decade or so of hard times, they were able to resume their economic and cultural relationship with Egypt. They regained their economic and cultural foundations. They continued to be viable, even prosperous. They maintained or recovered their economic and political clout within and among their hosts, which in turn allowed them to survive as a distinct group. They continued to worship their old gods, their traditional gods. They continued to hold themselves apart from the cultures that surrounded them.

Politically, and to some extent culturally, they had also separated from Egypt. Independence had been thrust upon them, and although they retained that economic relationship with Egypt, their survival had mandated relying upon themselves and each other - and not a Pharaonic administration far away. They retained their distinction from the local culture, but now were responsible for preserving and developing their own identity.

In short, they had passed a cultural threshold, a milestone, a gateway, whatever you call it, that ensured that they would not be absorbed into their hosts, would not vanish away, but would in fact retain and build on a separate identity.

And in fact, during the remaining dynasties of the New Kingdom, we saw the Proto-Cultists begin to diverge rapidly.

Gods are intensely situational. They reflect the societies in which they are found. Egypt had been a stable orderly society, fed by a stable orderly river, and protected by unchanging deserts. Their pantheon in turn was marked by an orderly stable of Gods, and a focus on correct and managed behaviour.

The Phoenicians and our Proto-Nabateans were from decidedly wilder and more disorderly contexts. The Phoenician and Mesopotamian gods were a quarrelsome lot, blundering, fighting, rising and falling, jockeying for power, giving and withholding favour. But they had at least the advantage that particular gods worshipers had local dominance, were the majority population, in a landscape that was known understood and predictable and that it was battles between centers of power.

But consider the environment of the Proto-Cultists. Their homeland was far far away, on the verge of receding into myth and legend at times for many of them. Egypt was becoming akin to a promised land, a land of dreams. And as relations with Egypt waxed and waned, the notion of a promised land took on a separate life, a separate land of dreams, or dreamland.

They were surrounded by alien strangers, who ruled an equally strange and unwelcoming land, and their livelihood was based on venturing onto perilous and alien seas.

Thoth, or Thoth-Kutbay immediately began to morph - his different roles driving him into different incarnations. There was the mindless violence of the sea, the uncontrollable, unpredictable chaos of the Indian Ocean typhoons and sea storms, the unpredictability of winds and currents. Thoth came to represent this, in conjunction with his Nabatean wife/creator deity, Aza. Aza-Thoth came to represent omnipotence, but a mindless chaotic omnipotence at the heart of creation.

Trade was essential, the lifeblood of the Proto-Cultists. Thoth needed to be the gatekeeper, the 'opener of doors' - it really was that simple.

Sea traffic was essential - so both Kutbay and Dagon became crucial maritime deities.

Ironically, Kutbay became the revelatory deity - the deity representing both exile and return. Kutbay would reside sleeping in paradise, originally accessible by sea voyage up the Red Sea. But eventually to be found under that sea itself, in a fantastic city of strange megalithic architecture, reminiscent of Egypt's great cities, waiting to eventually wake and call his devout worshipers home.

Kutbay would be dressed up in pseudo-Egyptian trappings, given aspects of maritime creatures, the body of a crocodile, the wings of a gull, the head of an octopus, all stapled loosely on the body of a man. His name would corrupt over time into Cthulhu. Nothing unearthly to any of it.

Dagon, the practical Phoenician, was stuck with the practical problems of getting from one place to another reasonably intact, and remained himself reasonably intact, although now distinctly fishy. He shifted from a god of wheat, to a god of the sea, and acquired a fish-tail, probably courtesy of Egyptian influence.

But the Pharaoh's expedition was far away from home. They were surrounded by an alien society, strangers in a strange land. Strangers whose tolerance they needed, and strangers whose trade they desired. They needed to go along, to get along.

The peoples that they dealt with were the Cushitic nations and tribes around the horn of Africa. The people who would become Somali's, Ethiopians, Oromo, Amhara and others.

These people worshiped a sky god named Waq, or perhaps Waaq. Waq would be supplanted by Islam, but would survive to be mentioned in the Koran. He also managed to survive here in the lore of the Cult. Waq is also pronounced Ioq, or even Iog or Yog. Does that sound familiar?

In Cushitic folklore, the term for supernatural possession, usually demonic possession is Zar. Usually, its unpleasant, demonic possession and all. But we can easily conceive a similar word to represent the joining or merging of deities.

Hence, Waaq-Zar-Thoth, represents the combining, perhaps simply the marriage, or perhaps the unification of concept of two gods. Waaq-Zar-Thoth through linguistic drift becomes Ioq-sa-Thoth, and eventually evolves to Yog-Sothoth.

It's here that Thoth eventually becomes two gods, as the Egyptian traders force him to straddle three constituencies. Azza-Thoth for the Proto-Nabateans of Arabia, and Waq-Zar-Thoth, for the Cushites around the horn of Africa, both of whom are critical, in their own ways, for the Egyptians.

The more worldly Phoenicians look askance at these developments, happy enough that Dagon is left alone and unpolluted.

And so, at this point, we see the core Cthulhu Cult Gods morphed into something we start to recognize as their current forms.

It did not happen overnight. For much of the New Kingdom, the Pantheon held relatively close to its Egyptian roots, the changes being one of emphasis and priority, and the marriage or incorporation of deities. But remote from Egypt, there was a steady drift away.

You can see it happening. Circa 1100 BC there is a community stele found in a Somalia dig which gives thanks for peace and prosperity to the Waq-Zar-Thoth - two gods who would become one in a few more centuries. There are papyrus records of prayers where sailors give thanks to Thoth for interceding with his mate Azza and saving them from the mindless fury of the typhoons.

Over time, this divided role of Thoth would result in two gods. Aza-Thoth, who represented the infinite - the sea, the storms, the wind, the chaotic universe; and Waq-Zar-Thoth, or Yog-Sothoth, the god of gates and harbours, the god of travel and trade.

Through the New Kingdom era, the Proto-Cultists retained strong ties with Egypt. Although doctrinally drifting, they had not outright broken with Egyptian religion or society.

Indeed, bits and pieces of Egyptian current affairs filtered into the Proto-Cultists emerging body of lore. We've already discussed the elevation of Nebmaatre Amenhotep to Nyarlathotep, and relegation of Akhnaton and his transformation in lore into the Black Pharaoh, of his capital, Akhetitan becoming the nameless and forgotten city, inhabited only by great reptiles.

But there's also Kadath, or more precisely, Kadesh, a fortress and the site of the great battle between the Egyptian and Hittite Empires in 1274 BC, recorded to this day by the Cult, albeit in distorted form. Apparently, it was a huge deal at the time, major news and with far reaching implications even at the other end of the black sea, worth documenting, albeit in increasingly distorted form over the years until little more than the name remained, attached to random fables.

The new relationship with Egypt endured throughout the balance of the New Kingdom, up to the Intermediate period, roughly around 1000 BC. It was a prosperous relationship for the Proto-Cultists. The Egyptian trade was lucrative. The Proto-Cultists made a lot of money, their travels and trading with each other allowed them to form connections, build relationships and make alliances.

They came to dominate the horn of Africa, forming a loose 'Pseudo-Egyptian' state, in which a tiny Egyptian/ Phoenician/ Nabatean minority dominated the population.

This dominance, maintained by wealth and influence, seemed solid, but was a house built on sand. The underlying cultures, the languages, the artisans and technology, the clans and lineages, and the social and ruling structures were intact and unchanged. These people themselves were not savages, but represented cultures as, or almost as sophisticated as their guests. The Proto-Cultists rule was essentially as thin as butter spread on a piece of bread. Their position was more akin to the Jewish folk of Europe in the middle ages, than the Colonialists from the modern age of exploration.

In fact, the rule over the Somali and Yemen coasts was always a fragile thing, with local revolts, expulsions. Wealth and trade intensified activity within the region. Local kings and empires came up, challenged or taxed the Proto-Cultists, who were then forced to relocate or fight back, to engineer assassinations, rebellions and coups, boycott and blockades.

The Proto-Cultists were a very vulnerable culture, but they had certain advantages. They were heirs to the Phoenician naval tradition. In fact, they did not just maintain but expanded on the Phoenician skills of boat building, sailing and navigation.

They were still local and coastal sailors. Blue water sailing was a risky endeavor, and they were traders not explorers. But over these first centuries, they developed an intimate knowledge of the waters and coastlines around Africa, the Arabian Peninsula and even the outskirts of the Persian Gulf.

This was their critical advantage over the local polities. Perhaps their only real advantage - they were the golden goose. They went far away, they came back with trade goods. Their trading activities manufactured wealth.

A local king might well have a trading post's members executed en masse, he could have them driven out, he could tax them excessively or mistreat them. But if he did that, well, there was a financial cost. He would lose the benefit of them. Indeed, that benefit would shift to his rivals up and down the coast. They would prosper against him. They might well become rich enough to come after him.

Mastery of the sea meant that they could leave if they were oppressed or unhappy. They could move opportunities, wealth, trade goods from one town to the next, depositing and withdrawing as to their advantage. They could communicate with each other from town to town, post to post. They could coordinate their actions, plan together and take joint endeavors.

If necessary, they could gather a war fleet, though there's no record of them ever doing so. The preference was always to hire mercenaries or manipulate others to fight their wars.

Ultimately, the Proto-Cultists were the worlds first 'Information Empire.' It was a communications empire, based on the movement of goods and information, and the selective control of that information, manipulating it, withholding it and disseminating it carefully.

Or perhaps it was the first multinational corporation in history, or a forerunner of the great trading companies - The Hudson Bay Company, the North West Company, the British and Dutch East India Companies.

Whatever you call them, the real threat to their future would not come from the host peoples who they lived and traded among...

Class dismissed.

New Gods, Tsathoggua and Ithaqua

Welcome back. I see that most of you are still healthy and hale. But there's a few missing faces. The weaklings are falling by the wayside. Hmm?

I'm sure we'll lose more along the way.

Simpkins, you're looking a bit green? Ha ha, just teasing you boy, think nothing of it..

Now, as you'll recall, we were reviewing the early history of the Cult, and its golden age during the Egyptian New Kingdom, when the primary deities began to evolve and consolidate to their present form.

The end of this golden age came around 1000 to 900 BC, with the fall of the Egyptian New Kingdom, and the commencement of what history has come to call the Third (and last) Egyptian Intermediate period.

Now, a word or two of the Cult, or the Proto-Cult at this time.

It is, it was, and it will continue to be essentially a merchant company. Perhaps a culture or coalition of merchant companies. But basically, they're traders. That's their reason for existence, to explore strange new worlds, to seek out new life and new civilizations, to boldly go where no Egyptian has gone before, to trade and bring back wonders for the Pharaoh. If part of that sounds familiar, well, it was an a hymn in an ancient text before it was a stirring motto for television space opera. Rod and Berry? Good cult name.

The religious aspect? That's unquestionably there. This was a pre-rational era. The world was full of uncertainties and mysteries. Things like currents, winds, storms, tides, all these things were intangible but vital. Everything was irrational and unpredictable. People did the best they could, but the supernatural, that embodiment of the unpredictable, and magic, that attempt to manipulate the unpredictable, was a real part of people's lives in ways that are simply not experienced now. It was a demon haunted world.

For a seaman, for a trader, for a farmer, the Gods and spirits were real entities, manipulating their lives capriciously. They were to be considered and second guessed, placated, entreated, invoked, occasionally cursed, often prayed to desperately, regularly propitiated and always acknowledged. So it was with the Cult, and the Gods of the Cult had been shaped to their particular needs.

And there was a vital unifying element. The people of the Cult, these Egyptians, Nabateans, Phoenicians, these peoples now cut off from their homelands for centuries, forced to rely upon each other, holding themselves apart from the peoples that hosted them.... To survive, they needed to bind themselves together, they needed a shared identity.

Religion and faith is often a core of social identity. It was a core for the Cultists, their faith constituting a shared identity for their far flung network. The Proto-Cult was evolving towards a formal Cult.

But it was not the thing, in and of itself, that it would be in modern times.

Now, let's take a moment and talk about trade.

The Proto-Cultist Trade, much like almost all ancient trade, involved transporting relatively small quantities of extremely high value goods. That's just the nature of the beast.

Transporting items costs money and time. Whether you transport by sea or by land, someone has to haul something from point A to point B. That's a costly endeavor. And mostly, you can't be sure that you will find a market or make a sufficient profit at the end of the voyage. So you have to factor that risk into things.

Which means if you are trading in 1200 BC, you are dealing with luxury trade goods: Portable, extremely valuable, with high profit margins. You are dealing goods to and for the wealthy.

This was the vulnerability of the Proto-Cultists, or the Cultists, as they were becoming.

Their society, their economy, their way of life, had been organized around servicing a wealthy and powerful civilization. A civilization with the spare resources, with the cash, to sustain a luxury commodity trade. That was the Egyptian New Kingdom. In a sense, around this period, the Cult is largely autonomous, but still dependent upon Egypt.

They're a loose kingdom or state or trading company. But their identity and economy is defined by Egypt. The Proto-Cult is basically equivalent to a tributary state.

That comes to an end around 1000 BC, and the close of the Twentieth Dynasty. By that time, the power of the Egyptian Pharaohs had waned. Economic troubles, subnormal flooding on the Nile, outbreaks and epidemics, and exhaustion from wars had weakened the Egyptian state, resulting in two defacto Egyptian kingdoms on the upper and lower courses of the Nile.

Over the next five hundred hears, Egypt would experience only brief periods of unity. Iinstead, the Nile was divided into rival, warring kingdoms. Sometimes several Egyptian states and city states coexisted. There were civil wars.

There were invasions. The Assyrians came in, roughly 600 BC, and sacked several of the major cities.

For the Proto-Cultists all this was trouble. Nothing but trouble. They needed a stable prosperous Egypt to make their living, and that's not what they were getting. They were getting a divided kingdom in a sea of troubles.

The chaos the Third Intermediate period was not continuous - there were periods of stability and relative stability. Nor was it entirely disastrous. If the Kingdom was divided, sometimes that meant that there were two Egyptian Kingdoms to be markets for luxury goods.

But it was harsh, and unstable. People didn't buy luxury goods during ongoing civil wars, during succession crises, during rebellions and famines. And quite often, the people who were experiencing these bad things were in the way of people who might have bought the luxury goods. Hard to reach your paying customers if you have to travel through a war or famine zone.

And of course, in an unstable and changing environment, the luxury goods that might be in demand might change dramatically, which added to the risk. Sometimes you made your delivery and there was no money to pay you, or worse, no survivors to pay you. That's hard when you're trying to run a business.

Overall, what this meant was that the Cultists might continue to make a living, occasionally even a good living, but it was more expensive and more unreliable, with more frequent crises.

What this meant for the Cultists position on the horn of Africa?

Well, unreliable, expensive and frequent crises was just not a good recipe for peace of mind. Or for stable business. The Cultists were a rich and influential Egyptian/ Nabatean/ Phoenician minority in a Cushite majority. They had achieved political dominance through spreading money around, buying allies and armies, bribing officials and the occasional judicious assassination. All this was contingent on having money available when you needed it. When you need to bribe a prince or hire an army or an assassin, the thing is, you need to do it 'now' - you can't do it on credit, and you can't wait until your investments to come in. If they come in.

So for the Cultists, the disruptions and turmoil in Egypt lead inevitably to disruptions and turmoil in their own corner of the world, in pogroms and expulsions, crises and civil wars, and disruptions of their own trading systems.

Indeed, with a little more pressure, perhaps the wrong crisis at the right time, we might have seen the political and economic networks of the Cultists fraying and disintegrating. They could easily have foundered, fallen apart, vanished into history.

Now, have any of you heard the phrase 'doubling down'?

It's a gamblers phrase. It describes the phenomena of a gambler continuing to bet, or even increasing his bets as he continues to lose. Basically, it describes an aspect of human nature. If something has been working for you... And its not working, or not working so well any more... the natural human tendency is to do more of it. It's also known as 'sunk cost fallacy."

In the case of the Cultists, the decline and instability of the Egyptian market spurred the Cultists to go further, to find rarer and more exotic and valuable luxury goods, to penetrate further into trade networks, to find and connect with new markets.

Explore they did. During the five centuries of the Intermediate period, the Cultists traveled further and further down the coast of Africa, establishing new posts and ports. They found their way to Madagascar, centuries before settlement. There is an Aepyornis Egg that's been found in a 25th Dynasty burial chamber, for example.

Nevertheless, the increasingly erratic and unreliable trade relationship with Egypt broke down completely in the period 670 to 650 BC, with the advent of a series of major wars and invasions by the Assyrians, who would end up pillaging the length of the country. Although this was eventually repelled and a fifty year period of stability emerged, the relationship with the Cult was irrevocably shattered.

The ongoing crises of the Intermediate period lead the Cultists to sail around the Arabian peninsula, encountering the Achmaenid Persian Empire, and beginning trading contacts there, starting roughly 800 BC. With the Assyrian wars, and the collapse of Egyptian trade, these new Persians were a godsend welcoming them with open arms. A parallel Persian oriented trading network was consolidated by about 660 BC.

This desperation to sustain the Egyptian market and to service the new Persian market during this period spurred further travel as far south as East Africa. It was along the shores of Africa that the Cultists acquired their next god.

Akuji, still remembered, though no longer worshiped, among the Turkana people of Kenya. Like Waaq, Akuji is a sky god, responsible for wind and rain. He's also the God of divination, of prediction and prophecy - and prediction and anticipation of rains is vitally important to the agricultural peoples of East Africa.

By this time, of course, the Cult pantheon is taking shape, and all the top spots for deities have been taken up by Azathoth, Yog-Sothoth, Cthulhu and Dagon. In his own culture, Akuji is equivalent to them as a creator god. But incorporated into the Cult, he is accorded a subordinate position

Instead, Akuji took on new significance for the Cultists and those they traded with in East Africa. Winds and rains were vitally significant to sailors, particularly winds. Divination, the spiritual guidance and predictions to navigate unknown waters, to meet new peoples, have a profitable exchange, this was vitally important. Akuji was incorporated into the Pantheon, becoming the vital god of Winds - the Wind Walker, the god of remote regions and luck. His name distorts from Akuji to Ithaqua.

During the same period, the Cult also explored and traded as far as the western coasts of India, during the Late Vedic period, beginning roughly 750 to 700 BC. Again, these contacts began to intensify after 660 BC, and within a century became well established. The Cultists came to be known as 'Men of Leng', and ancient descriptions of their dress and manner are very much those of Semitic traders.

It was with India that the Cultist finished their evolution - new gods were added to the Pantheon - most notably, Tsothuagga.

Indeed, cult lore references the Indian city of Sarnath, of which a spurious doom is written. Sarnath is well inland in central India, so it is remarkable to think of the Cult extending so far.

However, the writings of Sarnath in Cult lore, and the fact that the city is supernaturally destroyed. In reality, nothing of the sort occurred. Sarnath is around today, little worse for the wear.

This suggests that the city of Sarnath may have played a role in the Cult's politics or affairs in an unpleasant way. You don't write a 'and take that!' fable about people you don't care about, or about your friends.

The story of Sarnath in the mythos is that the people of Sarnath are latecomers to the area, initially living at peace. But soon enough, they rise up and exterminate their neighbors and are long after, eventually visited with divine retribution.

It's a typical story in religious texts. Sodom and Gomorrah, in Christian lore, and the fate of Irem in the Koran, are equivalents – God destroys a city of people who had it coming.

Note though, that in Sarnath, the sin of the people is not ungodliness, but murder. Specifically, the sudden rising up and purging an 'alien' population, an 'alien' population of arguably greater history and claim - they were there first.

It's not at all difficult to see this as a metaphorical history of a period where the Cult, after a century or more of success and stability in India, suddenly experiences a wave of pogroms and purges as a new cult or movement takes hold.

An interesting footnote for you all - Sarnath is known to conventional history as the city where the Buddha, Siddharta Guatama attained enlightenment. Buddhism was founded roughly between 560 and 490 BC - which would have been precisely during the period during which the Cult was expanding its relationship and connections with India.

So this raises the question of whether Tsothuagga - pronounced "suh-THOG-gwah" is in fact a distorted interpretation of "suh-DURTH-a-Gua." - Siddharta?

I will simply note that Tsothuagga is normally depicted as an obese, pot-bellied humanoid, often with exaggerated ears, much like certain depictions of the Buddha.

Don't be swayed by the animal attributes, this was a common practice in the Cult, derived from its Egyptian background. The Egyptians were always stapling animal parts onto their deities, and the Cult continued that hallowed tradition.

Tsothuagga is an interesting god in both its contemplative nature and its attribute of formlessness, its title as 'Lord of Oblivion.' This seems to smack of a fairly confused rendition of Buddhism. He bears all the marks of a new god, shoehorned into the pantheon, and with very strange attributes.

The stories of Sarnath and Tsothuagga suggest a fairly complex relationship between the Cult and the Buddhist faith. The incorporation of Tsothuagga as Buddha implies that there was a relationship, and some form of continued dealings.

But there are a number of indications that things may have turned rocky. In fact, relations went very sour, as far as doctrinal Buddhists were concerned. One of the Buddha's proscriptions, made in Sarnath, concerning the eating of human flesh, seems to have been an implicit condemnation of the Cult.

When you think about it, cannibalism probably wasn't a common practice on the Indian subcontinent itself, so there's no reason it should have occurred to the Buddha on its own.

But it was one of those folk tales frequently bandied about as to practices in far away remote and savage tribes, even in modern times, it was recorded in New Guineau and Melanesia. It was also a practical matter for the consideration of seafarers who were at risk of shipwreck and stranding, and who might be forced by desperation. For purposes of exploration and desperation, the Cult of this period did have some traditions dealing with the eating of human flesh.

And moreover, they were foreigners, and that was a common slur for faraway peoples. In medieval Europe, for example, it was an accusation frequently levelled against the Jewish folk – the 'blood libel' that they feasted on the flesh and blood of Christian children.

As with the Jewish folk, the members of the Cult, strange foreigners, travelling widely, coming and going, alien to the local culture, but living among them, earned a similar libel.

Which is why the Buddha chose to comment on it, and specifically to proscribe it. Without the Cult, it would never have been an issue. Siddharta's stance on cannibalism seems to have coincided with a period of persecution of the Cult in India.

Essentially, it was politics. The Cult had been there, Buddhism came along. At first they coexisted. Then at some point, the new Buddhist movement turned on the cult and purged them, leaving the Cult members with little else to do but flee with the clothes on their backs, leaving their worldly good behind and vow revenge, which vow turned into prophecy of doom, which prophecy eventually became the story. There are records of purges of Cult members in Sarnath, which spread to other communities.

So, if it appears that the Cult, in incorporating the Buddha into its pantheon, did him a disservice, it seems that there were hard feelings on both sides.

This of course is a recurring feature of the Cult. Due to its great antiquity, it will have its own record and referencing of historical events, often from it's own perspective, giving us a mirror universe view of events, many of which are themselves almost lost to history.

Ultimately, while the Cult explored further and further afield, the Egyptian relationship never truly reformed. Egypt would be overrun and under the Achaemenid Persian domination, after 500 BC. The Cultists needed to dance carefully, in prioritizing the interests of their new Achaemenid patrons, against those of their original founders, now unreliable, erratic and an Persian fiefdom.

Of course, a mere 150 years into the Achmaenid period, Alexander the Great comes along and disrupts everything all to hell, with succeeding Greek Dynasties in both Persia and Egypt. So the Cultists fail to stabilize as a sort of Persian tributary state in the way that they had been for the Egyptian New Kingdom.

Instead, they continue to evolve as a sort of trading company or trading league. But now, our Cultists have spread too far. The horn of Africa, the Red Sea, the African coast as far south as Mozambique or even the Cape, the Persian Gulf, the Indian coast, perhaps even the edges Southeast Asia.... There's no way you can maintain a state or a merchant company over those distances in those times. Not a state, not an organization, not a series of organizations.

The distances are so immense, the interests so specific, that the Cultist pseudo-state that once dominated the horn of Africa becomes attenuated, and what you get instead is a nationality, rather than a nation. You have a people, a religion, a lifestyle rather than a centrally organized entity.

So the Cultists become essentially the diaspora-Jews of the Indian Ocean. Or perhaps since the Cthulu Cult precedes Judaism, what the better description is to describe the post-diaspora Jews as essentially equivalent to Cthulu worshipers, except in Europe and North Africa, rather than the Indian Ocean.

One of the results, however, was that the control of the horn of Africa, the political influence that had lead to a Cultist 'state' became increasingly attenuated. They were still there, they were still powerful, but now the balance of interest and activity shifted elsewhere, centering on the Persian Gulf, reaching to India and Africa.

It is during this period, and in particular, following the collapse of the Achmaenid dynasty of Persia and the rise and fall of Alexander's Empire, that the Cult reaches its final form. This is when the principle or central pantheon and tenets become fully recognizable to us.

The Cult, by this time, is no longer a distinct ethnic people, or a concrete political and social unit. Rather, the religious aspect has become central. The Cult's membership has expanded. There are Indians and Persians in it, Cushites, Somali and Bantu, even Malay. The Cult has become a secret society, although one with very public assets. In almost every city and port, it maintained temples trading post, warehouses, counting houses and residences.

Keep in mind that the Cult was nowhere a majority faith. Everywhere it went, everyone it dealt with, it dealt as a small foreign minority. There were no cities or towns where it was a true majority of the population. At certain times and places, it might form a ruling class, even extend to forming the middle class, but even there they were vulnerable to their neighbors, to the majority populations of the lands they dealt with.

The Cult's survival and existence could not rely upon military force or demographic preponderance. Instead, it relied on knowledge: knowledge of sailing, knowledge of the seas, the currents, the distances from one place to another, and the travel times for getting to and from there, the knowledge of what lay in a particular place, of the local politics, of what was safe or not safe, what refuges were available nearby, of what was desired, what could be obtained, and where it could be taken.

Yet, this knowledge, as critical and as valuable as it was, was only half the story. The Cult was tiny. It was a small, thinly spread network, in the shadow of great cities and empires. The New Kingdom Egyptians, the Achmaenid Persians, the Greek Empires, even the smaller empires or city states of the

Arabian, African or Indian Coasts had the wealth and resources to build fleets of ships, the clout to push the Cult out of its markets by fiat or decree or competition...

If they had the knowledge.

In fact, there were efforts made. As the Achmaenid empire expanded, and its control over its territories increased, the Cultists found that much of their trading network was within the boundaries of the Persian Empire. Suddenly, the cosy relationship was less cosy, The Achmaenids empire found itself somewhat skeptical of foreign traders taking their wealth out of the state.

What to do? Open confrontation with the Achmaenids, or any local power, was suicide. The Cult's only asset was knowledge.

So we come to the other side of the information coin - secrecy. The sequestering of knowledge, its preservation and keeping it from outsiders. For that, a motivation deeper than money was needed, or some king or emperor would simply buy out those secrets. Secrecy and secret knowledge became the currency of the Cult, reinforced by religion.

Esoteric knowledge was wedded to practical knowledge, and forbidden to outsiders. Instead, knowledge would be doled out within the Cult, to the faithful, the trustworthy. Degrees and levels of faith and trustworthiness were established. Cult members could not simply worship and learn, but had to earn their way up.

It was quite a remarkable achievement - not only was there a system of both information and secrecy, but there was a pressing need to continually adjust and update that secret information, to sort it out, sift fact from fiction, wheat from chaff. Fascinating subject, and I would recommend those interested to next year's course - 'Before Cybernetics - Archaic Information Management Systems.'

Of course, once you have that system of information management - once you have your levels of access, passwords, authorities and authorizations, then you need some way to protect it and enforce it. Loose lips sink ships, and all it would take is one apostate Cultist bribed by a wealthy Emperor, and everything is put in danger.

So the Cult embraced the assassination business. Apostates, heretics, interlopers, blabbermouths? A grave would be found for each. Possible sell-outs would know what was awaiting them. Blackmail, kidnaping, threats and extortion became valuable tools. The Cult pioneered covert operations of various sorts. Misinformation both broad and selective was used to monitor for leaks. A not quite impenetrable veil of secrecy slowly and gradually settled over the Cult.

Everywhere they traded, they did their best to be good citizens, regular taxpayers, generous and fair neighbors. But they were also, and they had to be, utterly reticent and secretive in their ways. Those who inquired or pried could even be welcomed into the Cult.

But it was a one way trip. You could join the Cult, but on its terms, swearing to its secrecy, obeying its laws and hierarchies, and when you did... you no longer served the rest of the world. The Cult did not tolerate divided loyalties.

This turned out to be a very successful formula, and the Cthulhu Cult prospered and embarked on its own age of Exploration....

And that's enough for now.

The Unholy Transformation

We've said, that roughly 600 BC to 300 BC, the Cult reached a point of theological maturity - ie, the main pantheon of Gods, their principal attributes and relationships, and the overall structure and organization of the Cult was established.

This obviously does not mean that the Cult ceased to grow and evolve. Indeed, for the next 500 years, to the domination of Christianity in 200 CE, and another four hundred years after that, to the emergence of Islam in the 600's, the Cult had many ups and downs, many permutations. New gods were incorporated, schisms emerged and were quashed, the fortunes of the Cult and its members and incarnations rose and fell.

For those interested in the fine details, I will be happy to recommend some of our deeper history courses, reserved for third and fourth year students. And of course, there's much fertile ground for anyone considering a Masters Degree. But for now, we'll confine ourselves to some of the very basic themes.

The Cult had evolved from a dynastic trading enterprise, to a merchant company, to a pseudo-state, and then back to even more ambitious merchant companies - but by 300 BC at the latest the Cult had become so widespread across Africa, Arabia, Persia and India that no centralized or hierarchical authority was possible, it was simply too big, spread too far, with too many members and chapters, in too many places, with too many sets of interests.

The followers of the Cthulhu guides had become a religion rather than an enterprise. Religion was now the binding foce. Instead, what we had was shared foundation of practices and theology. Some of these practices may seem abhorrent.

Cannibalism for instance, seems abhorrent to us. On the other hand, cannibalism was the last refuge for lost or shipwrecked mariners and grave circumstances, so it was necessary to have some formal recognition and ritual governance as to when and how it was tolerable.

Human and animal sacrifice is also a theological response to exigent situations. Incest and inbreeding, and elaborate rules and permissions governing same were also developed and accepted from the situations of Cult members who found themselves small minorities in alien lands.

The 'feasts of flesh' the revels and orgies that 1920's and 1930's writers found so depraved? This was in fact a cultural response to prolonged absences as a result of sea voyages, with specific orgiastic rites commemorating both departures, arrivals and returns. Looked at in strict anthropological terms, it is no more atypical than Christmas, Easter and other equivalent holidays for agricultural settled societies.

Selective assassination, is of course a famous Cult trait - those who delve into its secrets or threaten its interests often come to untidy ends. This was as true in the era of Cicero and Pliny as it was for Mr. Lovecraft and Mr. Howard.

Finding themselves dealing continually with foreign and often threatening societies, the Cult evolved its own systems for management of information. Monopolizing information, enforced secrecy, and horizontal and literal hierarchy were all developed. The Cult employed a 'cell' and 'chapter' structure for its members. It recruited readily, but very selectively, and recruitment was often non-optional.

A hierarchy with series of levels of membership were established, with a basic level of sailors and traders, with access to wider and deeper knowledge and contacts, both practical and theological, as you proceeded up each level.

Indeed, the Cult's governing structure has been copied or reinvented by other secret or semi-secret societies, ranging from the Masons to the Scientologists. Really, they should pay royalties. Although in comparison, the rest of them are rank amateurs, stumbling about trying to reinvent lopsided wheels, where the Cult has long ago perfected the racing chariot... or perhaps, the Porsche.

The Cult from 300 BC onwards, entered its own age of exploration, although much of that was haphazard. Still, by the time we got to the Christian era, Cult's sailors had made their way around the horn of Africa, at least as far as what we now call Southwest Africa, or Namibia. Sadly, they found little engaging there, leaving a handful of ruins and some isolated settlements. They found but made little effort to heavily settle Madagascar. Their wanderings took them to Reunion, Mauritius, the Seychelles, Maldives, even Kerguelen and the Crozets. Indeed, they found almost all of the principle reefs. On all these Islands, they seldom settled, but often left remarkable ruins behind.

What were these ruins? Many of these islands were found reluctantly, the voyagers were lost, often castaways. They evolved a consistent architecture of durable structures that were half temples, half shelters/provision houses. The megalithic temples of Kerguelen are simply an extravagant example by castaways who never made it home. Tortoises and dodos were transplanted to several Islands as living larders.

Most of these island discoveries were only occasionally inhabited. The Cult were traders, not settlers. An island or island group that offered few trading advantages would simply be charted, a few temples would be erected just to be on the safe side, and abandoned.

The Cult maintained its own written language, a sort of mixture of cuneiform and hieroglyphics, but this was confined to the upper levels. Instead, the basic levels of Cultists evolved their own styles of picture writing, and often marked or inscribed their temples with elaborate pictorial stories, some of which offered practical instruction for survival, some of which simply told aspects of the Cult mythology.

The main emphasis of the Cult, however, was not erecting temples on godforsaken Indian Ocean Islands, but rather, trade - The Cult's commercial voyages took it steadily around the coasts of India, down into Southeast Asia, through the Indonesian and Philippine Islands, and even to the coasts of Australia and China.

Australia, of course, offered very little of apparent worth, so apart from a sprinkling of exotic megalithic ruins, and the introduction of a few animals, there's little of worthy comment.

China on the other hand, offered very different challenges. The Cult were avid traders, but China was an organized and orderly society, and a centralized one. It posed the same challenges to penetration as the Persian and Egyptian empires in their days, or the Roman empire of the same era.

Nevertheless, by the emergence of the Common Era, between 100 BC and 100 CE, the Cult had managed to evolve into the predominant trading network around the Indian Ocean, rivaling and challenging the famous silk road.

There were, of course, challenges. The Cult frequently found itself at odds with Rome, with Persia, with China, and with the passing Indian and Southeast Asian empires. Powerful states sought control and monopolization of their trade, and sought to capture and control revenues and influence. The result was a perpetual tug of war, and occasional hostilities.

 On several occasions, the Chinese state commissioned fleets to eradicate the Cult, including Zheng He's treasure fleet, none of which get very far or amount to very much. But it's the thought that counts.

The Cult had originally maintained a comfortable lead in seagoing technology. But of course, over the centuries or millennia, its traditional Phoenician derived boats and sail rigging would fall into obsolescence.

The Cult was forced to adapt and upgrade. But it also found it difficult to maintain a monopoly of sea technology. Other communities copied or even improved on its ships. The Cult continually had to adapt to circumstances.

The Cult's structure allowed for accumulation of capital, and the redistribution of some of that capital, in the form of a basic social safety net for Cult members. But also for accumulation of and allocation of some of that capital for venture projects, and the evolution of credit and debt financing systems. This lead at times to speculative bubbles, pyramid schemes, financial crashes, some within the Cult, some extending beyond. Entire states and city states blossomed and collapsed. But despite these reverses, the Cult fortunes carried it through times of trouble. It's proto-capitalism allowed it to outlast its rivals and competitors.

Superficial histories often posit the rise of Christianity or Islam as being instrumental in the Cults development. In this narrative, the Cultists are a happy community of depraved polytheists who are forced into an underground and covert lifestyle in response to Christian or Muslim persecution.

Well, yes and no.

In fact, the Cult had already acquired many of the key traits - the cell structure, the hidden hierarchies of knowledge and authority, the paranoid secrecy and information management, and the dedication to maintain both their information and economic monopolies, their subterfuge in the face of powerful societies - that allowed them to survive the rise and dominance of Christendom and Islam.

They didn't need to learn on their feet when confronted with the Monotheist faiths. They already had the tools and the lifestyles. They weren't driven underground, they were already underground. This is why Cult polytheism survived when its progenitors and predecessors - Egyptian, Phoenician, Mesopotamian, Greek and Roman polytheisms were all subsumed. The Cult was already a sneaky underdog used to surviving under the radar.

Now it's true that both Christianity and Islam proved aggressively intolerant of the Cult. Certainly any Mediterranean presence was eradicated in the early Christian era. But persecution was not perpetual and uniform, and even for Islam there were periods of grudging tolerance. The Cult was as good at delivering necessary or desirable trade goods, as it was for making itself invisible.

Indeed, elements of Islam, like some Buddhists before them, proved able to hold their noses, and deal with or tolerate the Cult, when it came to trade, or when it came to spreading the word of Islam. Islamic clerics were carried as far as Africa and Indonesia on the ships of the Cult. Let them travel the world saving souls, as long as they paid in cash.

Nevertheless, Islamic persecution, in particular, proved particularly fierce. The Cult's response to Christianity and Islam was to dive deeper, to become profoundly untouchable, and quite expert at subverting or assassinating as necessary.

Which takes us to the modern era, and the coming of the Portugese.

The Age of Infiltration

1453 was a watershed year. It marked the fall of Constantinople to the Ottoman Empire, and the final affirmation of Ottoman hegemony. It also marked the closing of the overland silk road. Europe was cut off from trade with India and China.

This is a gross oversimplification of course. There were a number of reasons for the breakdown of the silk road. But by and large we can say that the silk road was broken in the 1400's. For Europeans, this was entirely a bad thing. Europe, since the Roman era, had a desperate hunger for Chinese silk and for the manufactured products of the civilizations of India and China. Now they were cut off, and as the heroin addicts would say, they were jonesing for a fix.

The problem was that the Cult had been purged from the Mediteranean. Islam lay between them and Europe. For once in its history, the Cult failed to capitalize on an opportunity. The European market was left alone. Let the Europeans build their own ships and learn to sail, the elders of the Cult mocked.

To everyone's surprise, they did.

The result was the European age of exploration. It's no shock that by 1488 the Portugese had rounded the Cape of Good

Hope and were sailing into the Indian Ocean. Or that by 1492 Christopher Colombus, had sailed west to discover the New World for Spain.

For the Cult, the 1400's were a bad century full of tumult and reverses. The Ottoman Empire, with its domination of Egypt and Mesopotamia, the Persian Gulf, the Red Sea, and its ruthless application of discipline was an unwelcome development.

The Cult had managed to develop an uneasy coexistence, mutual understandings with the Arabs. That understanding did not apply to the Ottoman Turks.

In India, in China, in Southeast Asia and the East Indies, the Cult's fortunes had become erratic. Traditional markets and allies were becoming unreliable. It was a time of troubles. Perhaps the Cult did not take advantage of the opportunity to bring silk to Europe because they were unable to.

So, when the Portugese explorers encountered the Cult, both sides found mutual advantage. Both sides needed each other, each needed new opportunities and allies.

The Cult and the Portugese had several grounds for common cause. They had a mutual enemy in Islam. They had a shared interest in trade and wealth. The Portugese offered a new slate of opportunities. The Cult could offer the Portugese a literally detailed map of the Indian Ocean, complete with ports, cities, local contacts and connections. In turn, the Cult.... recruited.

Now, this isn't to say that Portugese explorers became, to a man, a band of slavering Cultists, complete with cannibalism, orgies and assassination. The Portugese were dedicated, even fanatical Christians. They had been part of the Reconquista which had thrown the Muslims out of Iberia. While not as extreme as Spain, there was no question as to their devotion.

And after centuries of Islam, the Cult had gotten very good at finessing doctrine and co-existing with intolerant monotheists. At the very basic levels of the faith, the Cult was even accepting of Christian doctrine, and simply incorporating its deities as saints, its traditions and customs, suitably adjusted for Christian consumption.

The sailors of the Portugese, far from home, in dangerous and unknown waters, for their own part were motivated to be tolerant and accepting, perhaps more so than people safe at home. If you are bound through the Indian Ocean, sailing weeks on end to strange and alien ports, and you're told that an Octopus headed effigy will protect you from cyclones and tropical storms... well, you're not entirely inclined to toss it overboard, particularly if its presented to you as somehow compatible and of a part with Jesus' ways.

Thus, as the Portugese made their inroads into the Indian Ocean and Asia, the Cult made its inroads into the Portugese, to the point where by the 1500's and 1600's, almost all of the Portugese sailors and fishermen, even back to Portugal, were to some degree either Cultists or Cult tolerant. Most considered themselves Christians, of course, just Christians with a little extra. And in fact, even today, you can find in many Portugese coastal villages, sigils, signs and representations which are traceable to the Cult.

Ironically, the persecution of the Jews following the Reconquista made it easier for the Cult to infiltrate and establish itself in Iberia, in both Portugal and Spain. There were economic and social niches opened which the Cult's traditions and customs were well suited to occupy.

From bases in Iberia, the Cult's traditions and membership expanded to both the Dutch and the British sailing cultures, although the infiltration was far from complete in those cases.

Both the British and Dutch repeatedly attempted to purge the Cultists from their sailing ranks. The Dutch were much more successful, to their regret.

The British had a better track record of knowing when and how to compromise. Overall though, outside of Iberia, the Cult made few inroads into Europe.

The real successes came in the new world, in Polynesia, and in the West Indies, where the Cult encountered fertile new ground or revitalized energy in its outlying territories.

And that brings us almost to the end. Next class, we ll take a look at the Cult in the modern era.

Cthulhu Today

And so we have come to the end of our survey of the Cthulhu Cult. What have we learned?

Instead of an ageless church of alien gods from beyond antiquity, we have a faith which precedes by centuries or millennia any contemporary religion - Judaism, Christianity, Buddhism, Islam. The Cthulhu cult is far more ancient than any of them. Its roots can be traced back to the earliest civilizations in human history. But it is part of human history, not outside it.

It is a faith of ages old gods, and yet a faith which has managed to flexibly adapt to changing circumstances. Nowhere a majority faith, it yet endures and spreads. It is a religion which has managed to establish itself in key economic and cultural niches which have facilitated that survival, which has evolved and continues to evolve and adapt and develop traditions which meet its needs.

I find that entirely admirable.

How many Cthulhu Cultists are there? A million? Ten million? Who knows? Do they still assassinate people? Well, officially no, but their enemies and investigators have a high mortality rate. Is it a worldwide central conspiracy? Or simply a particularly secretive but harmless faith? Is there even a central theology any more, or have millennia produced a diversity of doctrines and sects? There is much that is not known, or at least not officially known... unless of course, you sign up for the advanced courses.

So what is the status of the Cthulhu Cult today? Let's survey some of the best known regions of Cult activity.

New England - the Cult roots in New England go way back, as far as the original settlers. Cultists fleeing persecution established many of the communities up and down the New England coast - Innsmouth, Arkham, Dunswich and many others. The influence and power of the New England chapters of the cult rose and fell. During the New England age of sail and whaling, in the 1700's and early 1800's.

The Cult was so influential and powerful that Thomas Jefferson, diplomatically, would avow that the United States was in no way a Christian nation. The separation of Church and State was established specifically to ensure that the Cult would not establish itself as a state religion in some of the thirteen colonies.

The Cult also established a second bridgehead for itself in New Orleans - through its involvement in the fur trade, through the Cajuns, escaped slaves and oppressed blacks and through New Orleans centrality as an international port. The New Orleans and New England versions of the Cult maintain uniform theologies, but on the surface, they're as different as night and day. Let's just say that conclaves can get chilly.

The Cult, oddly enough, is not terribly successful in the Caribbean, at least not outside of Cuba. Heavily involved in the slave trade, and in mercantile commerce, it got squeezed out by a black underclass which saw it as predatory, and by a European overclass which preferred Christianity. The Caribbean is divided between Christianity and variants of Vodoun.

The Cult also made few inroads into Peru or Meso-America. The native cultures instead embraced a mixture of traditional ways and European Catholicism.

In Brazil, however, the Cults history with the Portugese lead to dominance. While Brazil is majority Catholic, it is believed that key sectors of society, including the ruling and commercial classes are either Cultist or Cult friendly.

The Cult, of course, retains its footholds on the Iberian peninsula, but has largely vanished from the rest of Europe.

In Africa, the Cult's strongholds are in the south, and on the east coast. It remains a potent, though covert, minority religion in India. It has numerous enclaves in the East Indies, particularly in Malaysia and the Philippines. It is common among Chinese expatriates, who are persecuted through Southeast Asia for that reason, and is a dominant religion in many Polynesian societies.

The Cult often has its strongest representation in cultural minorities. For instance, in West Africa, they were very widespread among the Hindu community. This was why in the 1970's, Idi Amin expelled all the East Asians. In

Indonesia and Vietnam, we see them widespread among the Chinese communities there, and consequent persecution.

But this is the tip of the iceberg - you can find isolated enclaves of the Cult anywhere that sailors go - every port city will have at least one hidden temple, and almost every sailor or seaman will knowingly or unknowingly bear at least one tattoo which can be traced back to the Cult's lore.

Did you know that in the 1920's, a tribe of Eskimos in Greenland were discovered to be Cthulhu worshipers? This had derived from contact with shipwrecked sailors a hundred and fifty years before.

The Cthulhu Cult is often accused of mongrelism - and in fact, it has always been accepting of racial and ethnic diversity. Among the Cult members, you will find blacks and whites, Malays, Polynesians, Aborigines, Spaniards, Indians both east and west, Filipinos - everyone is equal in the eyes of the Cult. Mixed race births are common and welcome.

Paradoxically, inbreeding is also common, as is a very careful sort of polygamy. The Cultists everywhere are careful to set themselves apart quietly from the general populations. They are careful to select their marriages among each other or among recruits. The result is that in certain isolated Cult communities, there tends to be .... unfortunates. Lovecraft wrote of the 'Innsmouth Look' as a signifier for the Cultists, but we find similar descriptions of traits going back well over a thousand years.

But with its worldwide distribution, with its long and complex history, can we even say that there is a Cthulhu cult any more? Or a that it is a single Cthulhu Cult? Perhaps like Christianity, it is now devolved into an endless litany of sects and splinters?

Certainly there is evidence of that. While the main gods and main theology is consistent, the New Englanders pantheon of subgods and practices is different from that of Brazil, which is different from that of Polynesia. The Cthulhu Cult incorporates, in aggregate, perhaps a few hundred gods, but not every god is widely recognized. It may well be that the Cult is perhaps more an idea or a movement than a concrete thing.

On the other hand, do we really know? Are there levels upon levels, in which secret masters of the Cult arrange the affairs of the world, move billions of dollars back and forth, direct assassinations, and steer the affairs of their worldwide church?

Again, these are questions for the advanced classes, which I'm sure many of you will be signing up for.

Now, looking at our attendance rolls, I am happy to note that our surviving class are almost uniformly of the faith. Except for Simpkins here.

Yes, I see you.

But no worries, I've scheduled an induction ceremony for Mr. Simpkins at the faculty lounge for this afternoon. Relax Mr. Simpkins, strictly wine and cheese, maybe a small orgy. The cannibalism part only comes into play if you try to flee.

And I assume you want your passing grade....

PART TWO
Lost Continents...Found!

The Fable of Atlantis

In western lore, there are three great lost continents. Atlantis, Lemuria and Mu.

Atlantis, the lost continent of the Atlantic Ocean, started out as an old fable from Plato. I'm sorry to say it never really existed.

Lemuria and Mu on the other hand, started off as semi-credible scientific theories in the 19th century. Spectacularly wrong scientific theories, but... science. Despite the fact that the science was wrong, it turns out that they they actually existed. There really were lost continents in the Indian and Pacific Oceans.

Atlantis was the original lost continent. It was a story told by Plato in a work called the Critias, around 360 B.C.. The story had legs, and was handed down through the ages. The Critias is a literary work, where Plato recites or recalls conversations he has had with various persons, including his friend Critias, whose name is used as the title of Plato's treatise about life, the universe, perfect societies, and ancient history. Critias relates to Plato the story of Atlantis, which comes down to him from his ancestor, Solon, three hundred years before, who in turn got it from the ancient Egyptians, who themselves got it from old records, and happened to mention it, because hey, Athens played a part.

As the story goes, Atlantis was this great Island kingdom, beloved by the Greek god, Poseidon, and full of everything from elephants and monkeys to gold and jewels. It was also home to a mighty empire, with a very detailed capital city. As things go, Atlantis got a bit too big for its britches, decided to invade Greece. The Greeks, lead by Athens, fought them off. The Gods, upset by the Atlanteans corruption, decided to sink Atlantis. The resulting tidal wave hit Greece and stripped it of much of its good fertile soil.

That's the brief version. You can go and find the original dialogue from Plato, and endless books on the subject. I won't bore you with the details. The point is, it's just a story.

To the cynical reader, there's a lot of details to the Atlantis story that tip us off that Plato was just having us on.

First, there's the provenance. Look at the way that Plato leads us into the story. Atlantis, he tells us, figures prominently in the history of Athens. After all, the Atlanteans invaded Athens, and then they suffered the wrath of the gods, which resulted in a big tidal wave denuding Greece.

Well, if that's true, it should be well remembered by the Greeks in general, and the Athenians in particular. But they don't, and it isn't.

Rather, Plato has to go into this whole song and dance about where the story comes from. It's told to Plato by Critias, so it's second hand, right there. Where does Critias get the story? He gets it from a legendary historical figure, Solon, so it's third hand information. Apparently, Solon's heirs have been keeping this story on the down low, in the family for three hundred years, before Critias decides to drop it on Plato out of the blue. Where does Solon get it? From the Egyptians, who apparently kept the records for thousands of years, fourth hand.

So this amazing story, where Athens is a vital part, and should be common knowledge for Athenian schoolboys, comes down as fourth hand hearsay, punctuated by centuries or millennia?

What's actually going on here is a well established literary technique where a bit of fiction is polished up by giving the story an elaborate imaginary history. The more incredible the story, the more elaborate the history of how it comes down to us.

If you read modern Sherlock Holmes stories, for instance, there's always this elaborate preface where it turns out that someone buys a wardrobe at an auction sale, and there turns out to be a secret compartment, which turns out to have a lost manuscript by Dr. John Watson, which turns out to recount an undiscovered Sherlock Holmes adventure. The 19th and early 20th century was just rife with this stuff, with manuscripts being found in bottles washed up on the beach, found in mysterious tombs, or pieces of furniture, recounted to scribes by dying narrators. Its just a classic literary device. Let's not pretend that the Ancient Greeks were ignorant of this little trick. They were out there inventing literature. They knew how to tart up a story.

There's more internal evidence. For instance, Athens plays a significant role in the story. A role that, if we were to take the rest of it seriously, is flat out impossible. Athens simply didn't exist, and certainly wasn't the player he makes it out to be during the time periods he asserts. No, Plato's just thrown

Athens in there as local interest, because his audience are all Athenians.

Then there's the deep and detailed discourse on Atlantean governance, engineering and whatnot. He goes into excruciating detail about how the capital city was laid out. I can't imagine the intricacies of foreign civic planning fascinated the Ancient Egyptians. I doubt that Solon would have cared much about it. And I don't believe for a second that Solon's grandkids were just on the edge of their seats over it. That's the sort of information that tends to drop out over time.

But it's exactly the stuff that Plato had a bee in his bonnet over. He was fascinated by ideas of perfect government, well ordered societies, idealized things. So this part of the Atlantis story is just Plato being a dog with a bone. He's just making it up, because he's really into this kind of thing, and the Atlantis story is such a good vehicle, he can't help himself.

Plato and his contemporaries told lots of stories, of races of dog headed men, of races of stork necked men, of men without heads but with their faces on their chests, of trees that sprouted sheep. According to the Greeks, gods showed up all over the place, getting involved in actual historical events. They lived in a colourful world, peopled, just beyond the horizon, by strange lands, stranger peoples and magical events.

A lot of this was traveler's tales, fabrications and fictions. Some of it was metaphorical or allegorical, some of it was mistaken, like the notion that women only had 28 teeth, and some of it was true. There were nuggets of truth in fantasy, big dollops of made up stuff in real stories. Troy seems to have existed. On the other hand, the Greek gods probably weren't throwing down on each other during the Trojan War. Solon was real. Hercules wasn't.

It was hard to tell which was which, and truthfully, in terms of the ancient approach to history and truth, it often didn't matter all that much to them. To the ancient Greeks and Romans, Alexander and Hercules were characters equally real and mythical. They were both, after all, long dead. It wasn't like they were going to kick down the doors and make trouble, as Persians were prone to doing. Nor was there money involved, as the prospects of trade with far off China might suggest. So why worry?

Atlantis, whether it had ever actually existed, was long long dead. As far as the ancients were concerned, it might as well have been history. What mattered now was its literary and metaphorical significance. The Greeks simply weren't all that troubled with literalness and details like actual historical fact.

Flash forward a whole bunch of centuries, and we're into the Renaissance, and from there, the age of enlightenment. Suddenly, people are counting to find out whether women really do have only 28 teeth. They didn't, by the way. The laissez faire attitude of the ancients is replaced by people who are making distinctions between fact and fancy, people for whom whether something actually happened is an important question. People were getting literal.

It was the age of Exploration. Ships were now sailing all around the world. Brand new continents were actually being discovered, along with new animals, new races of people, even whole new civilizations. A lot of stuff that people had taken for granted - dog headed races of humans, or giants, didn't seem to exist. A lot of travelers tales fell by the wayside. New things were discovered. Those distinctions, between the real and unreal keep getting made.

Atlantis takes on a new life. Suddenly, in the 18th and 19th century, it starts to be important whether Atlantis existed, or whether it was just a silly story. People were going 'okay, literary and metaphorical stuff aside, did it really exist? Yes or no?'

Partly this was rooted in racism. It was clear that the New World had hosted several advanced societies, including the Aztec, the Maya and the Inca. However, the European view was that the First Nations, the indigenous peoples were nothing but naked savages. Noble savages perhaps, but naked savages nevertheless. High civilizations just didn't jibe with naked savages. If the Indians had civilizations, they must have inherited it from somewhere else. Atlantis? It's not pretty, but there it is.

European and American settlers went to great lengths to figure out who was to blame for all those spectacular central American ruins. There were efforts to attribute it to the Phoenicians, to Egyptians, even to the Lost Tribes of Israel. Joseph Smith, the founder of the Mormon religion, came up with a spectacular story about good civilized Christ worshiping Indians, and bad uncivilized naked-savage, devil-worshiping Indians. As it turned out, Smith's bad Indians won out, exterminating the Good Indians, who left nothing but their ruins behind.

These sorts of theories invariably explained that those impressive civilizations had nothing to do with the people who were actually living there now, being enslaved or exterminated by generations of conquistadors and colonizers. Which meant, of course, that they were fair game. Hell, they even had it coming. There's always less guilt in wiping out savages than in wiping out civilizations. Such was the depth of social racism that it wasn't until well into the late 20th century that we began to realize that the Maya had not vanished, but were still inhabiting villages all over the region in which their dead cities were buried.

But anyway, a lot of these 19th century types were going to eat broken glass rather than admit that the naked savages had built all those pyramids themselves. The trouble was, there wasn't a good fit - the Egyptians, Phoenicians, Romans, Chinese, Lost Tribes just weren't up to snuff.

So Atlantis became the handy explanation - A missing lost land which was the origin of the American civilizations.

Or perhaps I'm being harsh. Sure, there was racism there, sometimes overt, sometimes subtle. And it was politically and socially convenient to attribute monuments to everyone but the locals. But Atlantis was a poetic idea with a long history, so it exerted its own fascination. The point is that in the 19th century, for various reasons, a lot of people got interested in the idea of Atlantis as a real place.

Finally, by 1882, Ignatius Donnelly, published "Atlantis: The Antediluvian World." It's a brilliant work. Totally wrong, of course, but still brilliant. It's probably the big landmark of crap science. But to be fair, the science wasn't completely crap. What Donnelly did, as did many of his subsequent pseudo-scientists, was assemble all the mysteries and anomalies he could lay his hands on, ranging from the strange migration habits of eels, the fact that the same or similar plants and animals were found on both sides of the ocean, inscriptions on rocks, Plato's story and Aztec legends, and stitched them all into a great overarching theory which explained everything through.... a sunken continent in the middle of the Atlantic Ocean! Nowadays, he would have just had his own 'Mysteries of the Universe' show on the History channel. Back then, he had to write a book.

To be fair, Atlantis was a decent enough working hypothesis for the 19th century. Although by 1882, science had pretty much already begun to pass Donnelly by. The only real problem with Donnelly's theory was that it just didn't hold up.

That's okay though. Frankly, that's the fate of most scientific theories. Most of what we've ever believed as science has wound up on the scrap heap, and more still keeps getting dumped there. Our civilization is basically knowledge sluts. We're fickle. Every time a better theory comes along, we ditch the old one.

Anyway, the cat was out of the bag, the Atlantis theory was on its way. From the 19th century on, every crackpot and visionary, and quite a few sober scientists had new theories as to where Atlantis was and what it was, ranging from the Azores to England, to the Sahara desert, Crete, Thera, Indonesia, Antarctica, Malta, Sardinia, Scotland, Iceland, the Caribbean, the Black Sea, the Bermuda Triangle. After a while, it gets easier to determine where Atlantis probably wasn't.

To be fair, there really are submerged lands. Between England and Denmark there's a lost Island called Doggerland, which was dry land during the ice age when water levels were low. The ice ages would soak up a lot of water into glaciers, sea levels would decline by hundreds of feet. There was simply a lot of continental shelf exposed everywhere. England was joined to Europe. In Indonesia, thousands of Islands were joined together in a land mass called Sundaland. The Persian gulf was dry land. But none of these places were Atlantis.

I'll tell you, if the Atlantis people and the Kennedy Assassination people ever wind up knocking heads, it'll make

English soccer riots look like a shuffleboard tournament. In fact, the whole thing gets so overloaded and crazy making that I'm going to stop talking about it.... Seriously.

But there is one thing that Atlantis started off that we'll play with: Lost Continents. You see, Atlantis enshrined in western thought the notion that there had been an Island, a land, even an entire continent that had simply vanished beneath the waves.

And where there had been one, there could be others.

Mu, lost land of the Pacific

Mu is often confused with Lemuria. Who would have thought? Actually, it just seems so logical. LeMUria? MU? Doesn't one sound like a contraction or elaboration of the other. It's an easy mistake to make.

Robert E. Howard, the pulp writer who created Conan, made a similar mistake, postulating a continent of Mu for his hero, King Kull, which later sinks resulting in the islands of Lemuria. Lin Carter's Lemuria is clearly derived from the same source. 19th century scientists and modern occultists manage to confuse the two.

Come on, they're both lost continents in non-European oceans bordering Asia and they sound practically the same. It just makes so much sense.

As it turns out, they're completely unrelated in any way. That's pretty amazing.

The handy rule of thumb is that Lemuria is in the Indian Ocean. It's about the Lemurs, right. Mu is in the Pacific ocean, think Moas or Moai (Polynesian monuments). At the very least, Australia and Indonesia stands between the two. Very easy to remember.

If some new age cult boy comes up and starts smooth talking your aura and offering to rub your chakras, and he just happens to mention Lemuria in the Pacific, or Mu in the Indian Ocean.... well, just spit on his karma, cause he's got a soul no older than a cauliflower and not half as wise. Basically, if they can't get that one simple fact right, then geez!!!

Anyway, Mu! As it turns out, Mu is an invention of the mid-19th century. Unlike Atlantis, it isn't the product of ancient fiction or more ancient legends. It's pretty modern. In fact, Mu also has almost as honourable scientific credentials as Lemuria.

What it was, was a bad translation.

Mu mostly is the creation of a pair of fellows named Etienne de Brasseur de Bourbourg and Augustus La Plangeon (not joke names).

A little bit of history is warranted. The Maya, possibly alone of all New World cultures, invented writing. And in fact, not only did they leave inscriptions all over the place, but they made books using tree-bark for paper. These books were called 'Codices' or 'Codexes.'

Of course, the Catholic Church was having none of this heathen writing. So they burned or defaced whatever they could. Which was almost all of them. Only three Mayan books, or 'Codexes' were known to have survived, one of which was the Troana Codex.

However, Diego de Landa, the Bishop of Yucatan, seems to have been a bit more forward thinking. He was almost as

diligent in making records of Maya culture as he was
destroying it. At one bonfire, he burned dozens or hundreds
of irreplaceable Maya Codex.

On the other hand, he made an attempt to create a
comparison alphabet, translating Mayan symbols into Latin.
Maybe it was for ease of witch burning, who knows. I think
his attitude was that the Maya script was not per se unholy, it
was merely everything they'd ever written which was an
offence to god. Perhaps on some level, he was hoping that
someday the Bible might be translated into Mayan script and
so spread the word.

It was far from perfect. It was actually pretty messed up. But
by the 20th century, we had it all sorted out and used it as the
Rosetta Stone to unlock the Maya language. Unfortunately,
19th century scholars hadn't sorted out the problems in the
de Landa alphabet (which was actually more a syllabary).
Hence, there were errors built in, and translations tended to
be hit or miss. Sometimes it would seem to turn out,
sometimes your translation amounted to gibberish. It tended
to be more art than science, and often more personal
projection than reading.

Fast forward from Diego de Landa to Etienne de Brasseur de
Bourbourg in 1864. He made an attempt to use the de Landa
alphabet to translate one of the Mayan books, the Troana
Codex. Unfortunately, he made the mistake of translating
numbers as letters, and thus wound up with "Mu." According
to Bourbourg, one of the stories the Codex told was an
ancient land, that he mistakenly read as Mu, that sank into the
ocean after a Volcanic eruption. It's not clear that Bourbourg
associated this with the Atlantis myth, although that's a pretty
obvious default. He might equally have been borrowing from
Aztec myths of Aztlan, which were better known than the

Maya. In any event, the notion of lost lands was hardly confined to Atlantis.

This brings us back to Auguste de Plangeon, our 'hero.' Born in 1826 he was a photographer, antiquarian and a bit of an amateur archeologist. It should be noted that there wasn't much of a gap between amateur archeologists and the professional ones in the 19th century. A lot of them simply figured it out as they went along digging things up.

Around about 1860, he started getting interested in the Maya and Incan cultures and began photographing ruins. Eventually, he produced a tremendous store of photographs, including of detailed records of sites which are no longer intact. In this way, as a careful and systematic photographer, he made a real and lasting contribution to science. On that basis, I'd call him a real archeologist for his time - Good basic work, wacky theories. You see it all the time in science. Better that than the other way around.

He was fascinated by the Maya, and developed a theory that the Maya had traveled to Southeast Asia, influencing the culture and architecture there, and eventually traveled further on to found the Egyptian civilization.

Even for his day, this was a wacky theory, given that it was pretty clear to everyone back then just how old the Egyptians were, and it was clear that the Mayans simply weren't that old. Hell, they probably weren't older than the Southeast Asians.

He wound up writing a fanciful and enthusiastic history of the Maya, alleging that they had telegraphs (the high technology of the day) and electricity, and even naming Mayan kings and queens. He divided the Maya into two groups, the classic Maya of the Yucatan, and much later Johnny-come-latelies who were Polynesian imitators.

Yes, Virginia, he was a bit of a crank. But he was an enthusiastic and well meaning one, and for once, his crankness didn't get in the way of his making some real contributions to archeology. So I'll give Plangeon a break. Besides, with a name like Plangeon, he's suffered enough.

Inspired by Bourborg, Plangeon made his own attempt to translate the Troano Codex. Unfortunately, he brought enthusiasm to the project, but not brilliance. And to be fair, the critical mistake wasn't actually his. With the de Landa alphabet, he gets "Mu" from Bourbourg's work. From this, he decides the "Mu" means Atlantis, although later on, he seems to have decided that it was a different lost continent in the Caribbean, and may have later relocated it to the Pacific. It moved a bit. Truthfully, his translation wasn't terribly specific as to where it was.

His translation tells of Queen Moo, or Mu, for whom two brothers vie. Eventually one brother wins the struggle, but darn it, the whole place sinks. Queen Mu then flees to found the civilization of Atlantis and then later Egypt. In Egypt, she's known as the Goddess Isis, and among other things, builds the sphinx. Ultimately, the survivors or Mu fled to the Yucatan, becoming the Maya, who then spread civilization to Atlantis, Egypt and Southeast Asia.

Remember the unconscious (or rather extremely conscious) racist subtext? A civilization like the Maya had to be from somewhere else. He's pulling it out of his butt, really.

But in his defense, he's working in good faith, and his mistakes are at least derived from the mistakes of older scholars. If he couldn't get the de Landa alphabet sorted out properly, well, I can't blame him. It would take another hundred years effort by more serious and smarter people with much better tools to get it right.

As it turns out, a proper translation of the Troana Codex reveals that its about Astronomy, and doesn't have anything to do with lost lands. The characters that Bourbourg and Plangeon thought meant 'Mu' were actually numbers. Think about that - Plangeon got that entire history of Queen Mu and all trying to translate an Astronomy text. I think he was projecting a bit.

To be fair, it wasn't that big a stretch. He was well aware of the Atlantis myth of Plato, and the Aztlan myth of the Aztecs. Just about every people have a legend of coming from somewhere else. Plangeon, in addition to the Codex, had been spending years around pyramids and inscriptions, and perhaps among the local Indians. It would have been very easy for him to innocently pick up preconceptions, make errors, or have European or Christian myths repeated back to him by the Indians, that would guide him in his efforts to translate a very difficult document with a flawed tool.

In hindsight, we can say that Plangeon read his own preconceptions into things. But at the time, his rendition of the origin story of the Maya, as being the descendants of sunken Mu, was not completely implausible.

Well, sort of.

Among serious archeologists, there was no actual evidence for Mu, and Plangeon's theory of a single culture inspiring both the Maya, Southeast Asia and Egypt, while it might have had an allure, certainly couldn't have happened the way he was proposing. The time periods for the civilizations were all wrong.

Still, there might have been merit to a 'Mu-ish' notion of a mysterious lost root culture inspiring the others. That idea might be floating around as something serious archeologists could debate. But Plangeon's theory was probably considered demented.

Ah well, just an observation to show the ideas were circulating. From an archeological point of view, there was a certain genuine plausibility to things. There were strange anomalies in the Pacific. giant megalithic Heads on Rapa Nui (Easter Island), a strange abandoned city on the Island of Pohnpei, massive stone structures in Hawaii, and of course all sorts of ruins on the Asian mainland. Lots of anomalies and strange things, not a lot of coherent theories.

Again, racism (not necessarily Plangeon's) reared its head. Obviously, the naked savages who lived on these Islands could not have raised the mighty stoneworks. Obviously, some higher civilization had come along, built these things, and then vanished. Obviously, other archeologists regarded Plangeon's wilder speculations with considerable skepticism, if not outright ridicule. But even a stopped clock was right twice a day, and Plangeon's theory or invention of Mu seemed to answer enough questions and fit enough facts that it wasn't dismissed out of hand. It sort of lingered on as semi-reputable, or 'kind of intriguing.'

It found adherents, even scholarly adherents who felt that there must have been a lost civilization in the Pacific, and whether you accepted the Maya or not, Mu was as good a name as any. So, like Lemuria, Mu was actually a hypothetical lost continent to explain oddities and peculiarities. A bit more dodgy than Lemuria, perhaps. But also with an archeological cachet.

And most oddly, the name Mu has nothing to do with Lemuria. It was invented completely independently.

Of course, just like Lemuria, once again, the lunatics got their hands on it. Why was that? Simple: Both Mu and Lemuria were completely blank slates. Look, if you were an occultist writing about Atlantis, well, you were stuck with what Plato had written. And Plato had written detailed descriptions of Atlantean history, architecture, geography and society. There wasn't a lot of room. It was stifling. Unless you were a crazy-ass psycho woman like Blavatsky, there was a sort of confinement - you needed to conform to Plato.

On the other hand, Mu and Lemuria had both begun life without any history at all. Both were merely largely blank hypothetical constructs invoked by the scientists of the day to answer some questions and bridge some gaps. Which meant you could invent any kind of lunacy and stick it in Mu and Lemuria!

And by god, they did!

The next big development in Mu came with Frank Churchward, who wrote an entire series of books about Mu in the 1920's and 30's. Churchward was either a raving lunatic or a bold-faced liar, possibly a bit of both. The point is that while Plangeon was as careful as he could be, his mistakes and delusions were honest, sincere and he actually made contributions to the field of archeology with his photography, Churchward was a different critter entirely.

Churchward's books, starting with the Lost Continent of Mu, argued that Mu was the birthplace of humanity, the original garden of Eden (an idea filched from Lemuria). It was the home of an advanced (but thankfully fully human) civilization called the Naacals, who existed 50,000 years ago, and who'd founded most of the other early human civilizations. The Naacals did pretty good for themselves, reaching a respectable 60 million population. Eventually, of course, their continent sank and that was it for them.

Luckily for Churchward, some of the Naacals made it into India or Tibet, where they were venerated as holy men and passed their wisdom and writings down. Churchward befriended a Hindu, who then taught him to read Naacal, making him one of three men in all of India who could read it. With that under his belt, Churchward then reconstructed the story of the Naacal from ancient manuscripts and legends.

Of course, Mu survivors wound up in other places, and left legends behind, so Churchward, now that he had the key to the language, could continue to discover lost Naacal manuscripts and, could decipher the truth behind these tales from related or derived neighboring civilizations, which allowed him to write many more Mu books.

My ass. There is no Naacal language. There is no Naacal writing. There is no ancient Hindu who teaches him to read it. Churchward was lying through his teeth, or he was in the grips of a major schizophrenic delusion. But if it is a delusion, its one that got him a lot of books published and a long term following and quite a bit of money.

Some people suggest that Churchward was influenced by Madame Blavatsky who also rambled on about lost continents as part of her Theosophy movement. It's entirely possible. She and her cult were certainly around blathering about Lemuria at the time he was writing about Mu, so its guaranteed that he would have encountered her ideas, and perhaps even read her stuff.

But I don't think its clear that he was borrowing anything from Lemuria (apart from the garden of Eden shtick which could have come through Plangeon or been independently invented) nor stealing from Blavatsky. Her writings were far more lunatic than his.

Instead, he seems to have relied more on the works of Plangeon. It's possible that on some level, Churchward confused Mu and Lemuria and regarded them as interchangeable, or one a subset of the other. But he was clearly going down a different path. Overlaps and confusion were inevitable, of course, but it does seem that we can identify clearly distinct intellectual traditions or pseudo-traditions in which, despite the confusion, the two places had different origins, histories, locations and confabulations.

From there, Mu took off. It wound up being popular in Japanese monster movies, Republic Serials, Pulp fiction and fantasy. Robert E. Howard and H.P. Lovecraft used it. Even Battlestar Galactica mentioned it. Like Lemuria, it was an exotic name to drop, when Atlantis was just too conventional and straightlaced.

Churchward's books sold well, and to his credit, he wasn't the loon Blavatsky was. But having said that, I suspect that his work thoroughly discredited the already shaky concept of Mu for the professional community.

The truth is that Mu's window of credibility, if it ever had one, was very short. The Mayan archeology developed and a clearer picture emerged. Plangeon's wilder notions were never really accepted, and they tended to undermine his 'lost continent' hypothesis, which was a few stones short of an actual foundation. Schlatter's Lemuria hypothesis, grounded in more careful science, seems to have lasted quite some time. Plangeon's theory was never terribly respectable and fell out of semi-favour quite quickly.

Meanwhile, investigations of Pohnpei, Rapa Nui and Hawaii demonstrated clearly that all the megalithic structures were home grown Polynesians. There was no origin myth, and there were no mysteries that needed solving. There never was a sunken continent in the Pacific Ocean. Except, as it turns out, there really was....

The Sunken Continent of Mu, Discovered

As it turns out there is a lost continent in the Pacific Ocean too. Go figure. It even has a name. Not Mu unfortunately. It's called Zealandia, which to me is just a terrible name, lacking anything resembling poetry.

Mu or Zealandia is a continental mass that's about 93% submerged. The 'non-submerged' part? That's New Zealand, obviously. Well, mostly its New Zealand. Another large extrusion of the lost continent are the Islands of New Caledonia, far to the north.

Obviously, we can see how the place got its name. And frankly, its just stupid. I want to protest. Where do I write? I mean... Zealandia? Jesus H. Christ! I hesitate to point this out but: ZeaLANDia? It's underwater! Truth in advertising people. ZeaSUNKia maybe. And really, they just stretched themselves didn't they. New Zealand... Zealandia, that's even lazier and more unimaginative than Lemuria. It doesn't sound like a place, much less a lost continent. It sounds like a fish store, or maybe a some place to buy draperies at a discount. Zealandia, the place down the street from Wal-Mart.

I don't understand this. There's a perfectly good tradition of naming real continents after imaginary ones. Australia was named after Terre Australis. America would have been named India, if there hadn't actually been a real India, but as it was, we just named the inhabitants Indians, and called the Caribbean the 'West Indies.' So, here we are, we've got a perfectly good imaginary Lost Continent, with an honest pedigree, and a perfectly fine name: Mu. And they went and called the place Zealandia! It's just terrible.

Hmmm. Where was I? Sorry about that. I get carried away sometimes.

Anyway, the Lost Continent of the Pacific: Zealandia (Which really ought to be called Mu). It is estimated to be between one third to one half the size of Australia (about a million to a million and a half square miles), not gargantuan, but respectable. Its much larger than Lemuria/Kerguelen.

Whereas Lemuria/Kerguelen was basically a volcanic growth, Zealandia seems to have been a real continental structure of tectonic plates. You can find it easily on topographic maps of the Pacific Ocean.

It's a weird looking, spindly starfish shaped thing, mostly composed of a couple of long narrow peninsulas stretching up from New Zealand, north towards Australia, a fat wedge-shaped ass dropping towards Antarctica, and another peninsula jutting out east. There's a couple of narrow ridges jutting northeast from New Zealand heading away from Australia that aren't technically part of Zealandia's geology. But in practical terms, we might as well include them.

Despite its relatively small size, it really sprawls. According to the Wikipedia, if it lay in the Northern Hemisphere, it would stretch from Haiti to Hudson Bay, or from Sweden to Sudan. This peculiar geography, as always, has consequences.

Zealandia originally began as part of the ancient Gondwana Southern Super-continent, that originally comprised

Antarctica, Africa, Australia, South America, India and Madagascar.

Geologically, Zealandia seems to have gone its own way relatively early, splitting away from Antarctica as early as 130 to 85 million years ago, and from Australia somewhere between 85 and 60 million years ago. Which raises an interesting possibility.

Zealandia could have become an isolated island continent anywhere from 130 to 65 million years ago, in the heyday of the age of dinosaurs. Which means that there's just a slim chance that the dinosaurs might have managed to avoid their worldwide extinction here, and hung on. It's a long shot, but you never know.

That's not as crazy as it sounds. There is a theory that goes that the asteroid that killed the dinosaurs hit the northern hemisphere. Didn't help the dinos in the southern hemisphere much, since the subsequent 'nuclear winter' got everyone. However, the theory goes that the dinosaurs of the south pole might have been adapted for long seasonal winters and polar nights anyway, and might have had the right adaptations to survive the 'nuclear winter.' That wouldn't have done them much good for Antarctica. But there have actually been serious searches in Australia, as the best extant location where they might have crossed the K-T boundary. The problem with the polar dinosaur theory is that while they could survive a polar winter, the wouldn't have any place to go. Eventually, the polar area was going to get very nasty, and they'd have to migrate somewhere even marginally warmer to survive, and there wasn't any place for them.

Zealandia is actually a better candidate. Not only would its southern reaches have been polar, and featured polar dinosaurs, but it's a much more sprawling, continent than

Australia, stretching potentially into tropical regions and with a lot more complex geography. If hardy, locally adapted polar dinosaurs had been there, they might have been able to migrate north to survive. Zealandia may have been their last stand. Of course, Zealandia sank twenty million years ago, so I guess when your number is up, its up.

Of course, if Zealandia separated from Australia 60 or 65 million years ago, or more recently... Well, we know that the dinosaurs certainly didn't make it in Australia, so they would have probably been extinct in Zealandia as well.

A later period separation from Australia, say 65 to 40 million years ago, would have meant that Zealandia was inheriting the same primitive stock of marsupials, monotremes and birds that Australia started with.

Mammals, both marsupials and placentals, both date back to about 130 million year ago in the area of China. They were successful enough to spread around the world, even into Gondwana. When Gondwana broke up, the new southern continents inherited the same kinds of mammals. Platypus fossils, for instance, have been found in Antarctica and South America. So we can assume that Zealandia's starting mammal baseline was probably similar to Australia's.

"Starting" being the operative word. Australia's modern marsupials and birds, including Emus, Kangaroos, Wombats and Tasmanian devils are the product of fifty or sixty million years of evolution. Zealandia would be beginning with a similar complement of root species, but they weren't guaranteed to turn into Kangaroos and Emus. They might go off on radically different directions. Indeed, the geography of Zealandia suggests things would have turned out very differently.

Its all about rainfall. Where does rainfall come from? From evaporation and condensation. What evaporates? Water. Where's most of the water? In the seas and oceans. There's just not as much water to evaporate on dry land, obviously. The truth is that most rainfall is coming from the seas and oceans, and usually falls there. A lot of the rainfall that falls on land is coming from water bearing clouds drifting overland from seas and oceans. This is why coastal areas tend to well watered and rainy, and while deep inland areas, tend to be dry or desert. If you look at most of the really big deserts, the Sahara, the Gobi, the Australian, or dry semi-arid lands like Siberia or the American northwest, they tend to be far inland.

It's also why geography is so important. Australia, which is basically a big round lump has a vast interior desert. Europe, roughly the same size and very squiggly geography is much nicer. Look carefully at Europe, its all peninsulas - Italy, Iberia, Scandinavia, the Balkans, wrapped around by seas, including the Adriatic, the Aegean, the Baltic, the Black, the Channel, the Irish, the Mediterranean, the North Sea. There's very few places in Europe which are more than a few hundred miles from the sea. The result is that Europe gets a lot more water in a lot more places than Australia, and it doesn't have a significant desert anywhere.

There's more to it. Hills and mountains are vital. See, clouds just go where the breeze takes them. But when clouds meet up with mountains? Well, those things are just too high, the really heavy water bearing clouds can't go over them. The clouds just kind of stop there, piling up like sheep at a fence. Eventually they end up getting so thick and crowded that they release their water, and you get a lot of rain. So one side of the mountain range ends up pretty wet with lots of rainfall. The other side ends up pretty dry. On the wet side, that rainfall collects, winds up turning into rivers and lakes, and so you've got nice drainage basin forming, which produces good farmland or a tidy little rain forest. Most of the worlds great rivers can be traced to mountain ranges.

Unless it's a sort of box, mountain ranges will block clouds and wind but it won't stop them. Clouds slide along the ranges, releasing their water, moving back and forth. If you've got curves or loops, or a few extra mountain ranges going in different directions and angles, the clouds get shuffled along, sort of like a slow motion pinball, or really fast lines at the DMV. So you've got a lot of rainfall, which ends up in your lowlands and valleys, all sorts of interesting things happen. Windbreaks tend to mean air doesn't move around as much, so heat gets trapped, it gets warm. The bottom line is that complicated geography makes Europe a pretty nice place to live, while uncomplicated geography makes places like the Sahara and the Australian outback not so nice. So, where does this all come back to? Zealandia, of course. Let's take another look.

Zealandia goes high and long. It's all narrow peninsulas with long central hill or mountain ranges. Those are rain traps galore. Zealandia, or Mu, is going to get a lot of rain. Rain of course is good for vegetation. So Zealandia is going to be a continent chock full of rain forests and vegetation. The cooler latitudes will be like British Columbia, the warmer ones will be like the Amazon or the Congo. The point is, lots and lots of trees, lots and lots of rivers and streams. Probably in the lower lands, you get lots of lakes, marshes and swamps. After all, there's a lot of water coming down everywhere. Even if a lot of it drains back into the ocean, there'll be places where it collects into lakes. This is, after all, complicated geography. Complicated geography and mountains gets you lakes.

Shallow lakes or low geography gets silt draining into the rivers and lakes, which gets you marshes and swamps.

So, what does this mean for Zealandia's life forms? Well, lots of birds obviously, and lots of kinds of birds. They do well with trees. It's that whole living in three dimensions thing. So, parrots, woodpeckers and everything in between. And for mammals, lots of tree climbers - basically, we'll see all sorts of marsupial equivalents of squirrels and lemurs and raccoons, probably sloth-analogs, even things that might resemble monkeys and apes. Possibly some tree-climbing cats.

There are size limits on tree life, of course. The bigger you are, the fewer branches its safe to climb around on and the more dangerous a fall becomes. The orangutang is the biggest tree dweller around at 200 pounds and its kind of a freak, so we can safely say that they represent the absolute upper limit. Most tree dwellers will be a lot smaller. The upper range of sloths and gibbons seems hefty. You'll see most of your birds and animals in the range between a few ounces and fifteen pounds.

Larger animals will tend to be on the forest floors. We can get some fair sized critters: Deer and moose, tapirs and boar. But the herbivores probably won't get much larger than that. For the really big bruisers, like bison, or rhinos or elephants, or for big herds, you'll generally need open country. Hmmm. Scratch that. Elephants aren't normally considered deep rain forest creatures, but they do tend to inhabit the outer forests and brushlands. So you might get some healthy sized creatures on the forest floor, depending.

You might see specialized adaptations for getting around and feeding: Trunks, tusks, long hooked claws, long limbs. The forest floor is ecologically a rich zone, so you'll see burrowers, diggers and rooters. Probably there will be creatures equivalent to pigs and badgers. A wealthy, biologically rich, environment produces specialization, so we might see some very peculiar creatures with very odd specialized adaptations.

Of course, you'll see predators. Most likely, given the conditions, they'll be solitary ambush predators. There aren't the herds to support prides or packs of predators, nor the open spaces that require them to work co-operatively. Instead, there's lots of cover to hide in and burst from. So instead of wolf or lion analogs, the more likely critters will be tiger and sabertooth copies. Given the likely diversity of small life forms, squirrel types, we probably won't see that many big predators hunting big game. Most predators will be small-critter hunters. The environment is rich enough and diverse enough in food sources that we might see creatures in ecological niches similar to bears. Or we might see extremely specialized predators with peculiar adaptations, something like anteaters.

The marshlands and rivers are likely to be a series of major regions. So we're likely to see equivalents to platypus, beavers, muskrats, otters, all the way up to moose and hippos. The warmer latitudes nearer the equator will be hospitable to crocodiles.

On the other hand, probably not lots of grasslands. Oh, certainly there will be plains and grasslands. New Zealand has them now, and Mu is about twenty times bigger. But nothing equivalent to the American prairie, the Asian Steppe or the African Savannah (each of which were as large or larger than the entire continent of Mu). Australia, when it was wetter had something close to those open ranges, and to some extent, still does. So it evolved specialized open country critters - kangaroos. Other open country creatures North America,

Asia and Africa included bison, pronghorns, aurochs, horses, antelope, zebras, elephants, giraffes, etc.

Kangaroos or bison are pretty unlikely here. Rather, the plains and grasslands will be inhabited by emigrants from the forest floor, and they won't be particularly well adapted for the grassland. Hoofed runners or hoppers will be unlikely, herbivores will be slow moving and heavy footed, even on the grasslands. The big difference might be heavier heads and jaws to chew tougher grassland plants. For good runners, you want lots of open grassland. If the herbivores can't flee, then they'll probably be fighters, so tough muscular critters, likely with businesslike horns or tusks.

We can pretty much forget about deserts in Mu. Not with that geography. The closest you'll find are a few dry spots on the wrong sides of mountains. But the continent is so narrow and twisty that, like Europe, there won't be many of those.

On the other hand, what you might find are hill and mountain specialists - rock climbers, cliff dwellers, equivalents to mountain goats. You might find, for instance, ape or sloth like creatures that spend their entire lives living on cliff faces. Or you might find semi-aquatic fishers who live exclusively above or below waterfalls, gripping tightly with their limbs and spearing or grabbing fish trapped in current or stunned by falls with long flexible necks, long jaws, trunks or tongues. And you'll probably find hill or mountain micro-ecologies.

What we probably won't get anywhere, are giants. There's a reason for that. You see, for bigger and bigger critters, you need bigger and bigger habitat. Basically, a larger animal needs more territory to feed. A viable population of them therefore needs a much bigger territory. And of course, being bigger usually means slower growing and longer lived, so you need a bigger territory to be stable for a long time. Which means it takes a lot longer to evolve, and you need that big stable territory to stay there for a while. The bottom line, you don't get elephants or elephant sized critters evolving in Europe or Australia. The biggest fauna of these places, while hefty, was just not in that size range.

It's true that giant sloths evolved in South America, and mammoths made a go of it in North America. But where are they now? The biggest animals currently in North or South America make do with being cattle sized - tapirs, musk ox, moose and bison. Island populations can produce giants of course. The moas reached fifteen feet in height and a few hundred pounds. The Madagascar bird reached a thousand pounds and the biggest lemur probably hit 600. But then again, these are only comparative giants. A range between 500 and 1000 pounds, while impressive, is only really about the range of cattle.

Now, the thing with Mu is that while it's a big place at a million and a half square miles, its also spreading out thinly across a lot of latitudes. Different latitudes bring different temperature levels, ranging from cool temperate to steaming tropical. The frequency and periodicity of rains will vary. The cooler latitudes might have continuous rain. The warmer ones might have rainy and dry seasons. The amount of day and night will vary with the latitude. And the presence of seasons may vary, with tropical regions having possibly no apparent season, while cold latitudes might have very strongly distinct seasons. This means that the mixture of plants and resources, and the species, will change as you move north and south. And because Mu is essentially nothing but long comparatively narrow peninsulas, this means that the habitat in a given set of latitudes will tend not to be very big in comparison to similar habitats at similar latitudes in South America, Asia or Africa. Or even, for that matter, Australia.

Smaller habitats = smaller critters. Its just that simple. Probably no giants.

Of course that's just a guess. We might, for instance, have very big generalized omnivores moving on seasonal migration routes up and down the coasts, just like bison. Migratory animals tend to be bigger because they're not confined to a local food source, just compare the size of stay at home pigeons to wandering Canada geese. But the Muan environment, tropical and wet, would be a lot richer than the American plains that support bison, so you might actually have pretty gigantic migrators, possibly on elephant level size scales. Unlikely, but possible.

As to what Muan megafauna might look like, that's pure speculation. At that size, massive thick legs, heavy bodies. But after that? It might have trunks like elephants, long spindly figures like giraffes, or huge curving hooked claws like giant sloths, or heavy bodies like hippos. It's unlikely that you'd get a marsupial version of a sauropod dinosaur, mammals seem to have a fixed number of neck bones, which is why giraffes are so stiff necked. On the other hand, I could see scaling up a creature like a wallaby or kangaroo until it was the size of an iguanodon or bigger. I could even imagine an ape-like creature going King Kong sized. Or possibly something as uninteresting and unstylish as a diprodont or tapir.

The diversity of habitats and the small habitat size across a series of latitudes tells us a bit about the sort of life we'll encounter. Likely at the smaller sizes, we'll see lots of speciation and specialization.

Think squirrels. In North America, we've got pretty much the same trees and tree populations over large areas, so we get only a few species of squirrels. Moreover, the habitats of the few main species of squirrels are so large that their populations simply overwhelm the more narrow or specialized habitats that might have lead to different squirrel species.

In Mu, it'll be completely the opposite, lots of small little habitats encouraging specialization, with no big reservoir to overwhelm the small fry. So in Mu, we'll see hundreds of kinds of squirrels-types for instance, and we'll see weird squirrels. We'll see flying squirrels, and honey squirrels, carnivorous egg stealing squirrels, or whatever you can imagine. The larger animals, on the other hand, will tend to be more generalized, more flexible, more adaptable, to extend their range across latitudes and habitats. So there'll be relatively fewer species of Mu kangaroo or antelope equivalents. Some of the most versatile species might range from one end to the other. But mainly, it's a continent of long skinny penininsulas, so there's going to be a lot of localization and local varieties of everything.

But, let's hold on a second here. We've been assuming that the fauna will start from the same stock as Australia - mammals, even if they are marsupials and monotremes. New Zealand has no mammals. It's an island of flightless birds. So shouldn't we simply be talking about a continent of flightless birds? More and more and bigger and bigger and weirder and stranger Moas? Perhaps instead of Mu we should call it Mo? Good point.

Giant flightless birds, all seem to derive from the ancient southern supercontinent that included Africa, India, South America, Australia, Madagascar and the Zealandia continent. They seem to have gotten their start before the supercontinent broke up, before the dinosaurs punched their ticket. So its pretty much a lock that, no matter what else survived in Mu, we would have seen either Moa or perhaps more robust relatives of Moa.

But here's an interesting thing: New Zealand has no native mammals now. But in 2006, fossils were discovered for a native mouse-like mammal that lived as recently as 16 million years ago. Now there's a puzzle. What happened to the mammals?

I never used to worry about this. I just figured that New Zealand was a geological freak, something like Iceland. I thought it had been created by a fold in the earth's crust, or the product of volcanic uplift, and it had never been connected to anything and therefore, it had never had mammals, just birds flying in.

But I was wrong in two respects: New Zealand was part of a continent, and a continent that had been connected to other continents. So clearly, mammals were getting there. And those mammals had survived until as much as 45 million years after the separation of continents. So what was going on? How could flightless birds establish themselves. Why didn't the Gondwana mammals overrun all the niches and diversify, like they did in South America and Australia and just about everywhere else? Why weren't there more of them? And why did they seem to die out without accomplishing anything?

The only thing I can think of is that the mammals got unlucky. Something happened to New Zealand, glaciations or volcanic disasters, that wiped them out, or left their populations so reduced and confined that they could not compete with the birds.

Given that 93% of Mu is sunken today, its tempting to speculate that some of modern New Zealand itself spent some time underwater. Perhaps a few times. That would have wiped the islands clean of most mammal species, perhaps all of them. Plants might have survived on higher islands, or uplands, to recolonize the rest of the landscape when New Zealand rose up again. Any mammals that survived on the vestigial Islands might have simply been 'boxed' species, too specialized to be able to take advantage of opportunities and move out of their niches. The populations may have simply been vulnerable to change and eventually lost out.

Alternately, we know that New Zealand was affected by and partially glaciated during the ice ages. So perhaps the ice age got them. Not impossible. Its hard to live underneath or on top of a glacier. Even if you weren't glaciated under, the cold weather might have made it very hard for small semi-tropical mammals to survive. Bigger mammals could have weathered the cold, but perhaps not the change of diet as warm temperature plants died off. Larger animals were probably more specialized, so a reduction in plant life or a major change of diet could well have done them for.

That's the trouble with living on an island. On a continent, you can always just move, there's almost always some place you can retreat to - north, south, east, west, up or down. On an Island, sometimes there's no place to retreat, your back goes up against a wall and suddenly, zap, you're extinct. Bummer.

Of course, even a continent can be too small sometimes. The mammoths and giant sloths can tell you that. Sometimes the Earth itself isn't big enough, as the dinosaurs found out. Let's hope humanity doesn't learn the same ugly lesson.

But that's New Zealand. If we were talking Mu, then the mammals could have simply retreated back to the warmer latitudes and waited out the ice age. In which case, our examination of Muan life holds up.

If on the other hand, it was a submergence, then we have to accept the notion that the entire continent could have temporarily submerged, as its mostly submerged now. In which case, we are wiped clean of all the exotic possibilities in Mammals, and work with exotic new possibilities: It's moas all the way down!

Okay, let's move on. Supposing that Mu had not submerged. Or supposing that it had re-emerged. How would it have affected history? What's the alternate history?

What if Mu Never Sank?

Here's a bit of speculation...

In our timeline, Australia and New Zealand were pretty obscure places. Australia had been discovered and settled by the people who would become Aborigines about 40,000 years ago. And then they seemed to drop right out of history. Everyone forgot about Australia for about 40,000 years. There were no significant new waves of colonization, not even by the Malay who settled Madagascar an ocean away, or by the Polynesians who ventured across the Pacific Ocean. It was as if Australia was a great big blind spot. If anyone found it in the subsequent millennia, no one apparently wanted it.

New Zealand remained entirely undisturbed. Humanity did not discover and colonize it until approximately 800-1300 AD, during the last bursts exploration of the Polynesian seafaring civilization.

So, theoretically then, Mu might have been an undiscovered country? To have been unoccupied, unknown, until

Maori/Polynesians in their wave of expansion in the last thousand year.

Not quite.

The northern extremity of Mu is represented now by the islands of New Caledonia, and they have a complex history. The colonists of New Caledonia were called the Lapita people, an Austronesian culture believed to have originated in Taiwan or possibly the Bismarck Archipelago, sometime between 50,000 and 10,000 years ago.

Somehow, in the period between approximately 4000 and 1000 years ago, the Lapita culture, evolving into the Polynesians, underwent an astonishing age of exploration and colonization. They show up in New Caledonia around 1500 BC. They reached the Bismarck Archipelago and Samoa by at least 1350 BC, Tonga and Vanuatu by 1000 BC. They crossed the Pacific, finding every significant island. They made it to Hawaii and Easter Island by 300 AD, New Zealand by 800 AD. They managed to sail across a quarter of the Earth's surface in an era when practically no one else ventured out of sight of land.

New Caledonia, the most northerly outpost of sunken Mu, was settled about 3500 years ago. Ancient, but not necessarily super-ancient. 3500 years ago there were quite a few civilizations developing nicely, including the Babylonians, the Egyptians, the Indus cultures, China etc.

Sea colonization takes a fair bit of cultural sophistication. Undertaking sea voyages to places like New Caledonia, Fiji and Tonga that meant they had to be skillful at building and provisioning huge canoes for long voyages. More than simple provisioning, their canoes literally had to be 'space-ships' carrying women and children, domestic animals, plants and seeds, and the full roster of tools necessary to recreate their society in a foreign land far far from home.

Building and maintaining such boats required an advanced and sophisticated toolkit of wood cutting and shaping tools. It required multiple raw materials, weaving, mastery of fibres and fire making. It also required substantial knowledge of stars, currents, navigation and weather. The Lapita culture featured several domesticated animals, including pigs, chickens and dogs. They'd mastered root and tree crops, including taro, yam, coconut, bananas and breadfruit as well as being sophisticated offshore and deep sea fishermen.

Repeatedly, the Lapita/Polynesian culture reached remarkable heights. On Easter Island they built megalithic sculptures and perhaps invented a form of writing. On Pohnape an offshore city was built. On Hawaii immense structures were engineered. On Fiji and Tonga, in Hawaii, on New Zealand, the Lapita, the Polynesians or the Maori fought wars and built empires. They were a sophisticated, adventurous, innovative people.

Over and over again, the only limitation on their culture was the geographical and population limitations of the islands that they lived on. Give a people like that an entire Continent to play with.... Well, who knows what they might do?

So, assuming that the Lapita/Proto Polynesians found Mu, which is pretty much a given, since they found New Caledonia, then what happens?

Well, first things first: Colonization of the entire continent, starting from New Caledonia and working their way down. Multiple settlements founded. Possible extinctions of domestic fauna, but probably not that much. Forest types are much more resilient and resistant to extirpation than open country animals.

On the other hand, rich soils, lots of rain and warm weather mean that the Muans will find agriculture very rewarding. In addition, the seas around Mu are shallow, which makes for good fishing. High food productivity means increasingly dense populations. Villages become towns, towns become cities.

The new Muans will hang close to the sea or rivers and sailing will continue to be important to them. For one thing, they have no beasts of burden - no oxen or horses. (It's possible that they may be able to domestic indigenous animals as draft animals, or that at some later point in their history they obtain horses or oxen from Asia or Indonesia). This means that transporting cargo will be done by water whenever possible. Also, the peculiar layout of Mu, all peninsulas and mountain ranges, means that if you want to get anywhere its usually far easier to take a boat than go overland. To make life a little easier, the Muans may dig canals or build harbours. With more wood sources, their boat building gets more sophisticated, and they develop rafts and barges for bulk movement, small canal shippers, etc.

Inevitably, Mu is far too large. Different communities or city states begin to emerge. There is regular contact through trade, exchange and competition. The domestication or acquisition of draft animals expands agriculture, expanding local populations. An Age of City states begins, perhaps analogous to the Greek or Phoenician eras of City states. Out in the Pacific vast distances amounted to a barrier between competing Lapita/Polynesian cultures. Here, large communities jostle up against each other easily. We can imagine war, breakneck development, social experiments, a flowering of culture, philosophy, art and science, and Empire building. Of course, no one City State can manage to sequester the population and resources to overwhelm the others. So Mu remains an uneasy collection of city states.

Australia is discovered. Probably, it's discovered quickly. Both the ancestral Lapita and the Muans are dedicated sailors, and Australia is not that far from Muan peninsulas. Australia, in this alternate universe, actually does a lot better geographically with the Muan continent adjacent. Rain clouds, instead of drifting east and pouring out into the ocean, are now funneled between the two continents, resulting in the eastern coast of Australia receiving more rainfall, and receiving rainfall deeper into the interior, producing a biologically richer and more productive region.

Central and Western Australia is largely unchanged, being pretty much a desert. The Muans establish colonies on the Australian coast which become City States on their own, much as the Phoenicians and Greeks established colonies in the far reaches of the Mediterranean. The original inhabitants, the Aborigines, are pushed out or enslaved. Meanwhile, the Muans explore the coastlines of Australia, finding Tasmania and New Guinea and eventually entering the Indian Ocean.

There may be trade with the cultures of Asia, beginning with Indonesia, extending up Southeast Asia, and as far as China and India. There may be a second wave of ocean exploration and colonization, in both the Pacific and Indian Oceans. The Muans find the major island groups, the Marquessas, the Cook and Cocos, Reunion, Mauritius, Andaman and Nicobar, Maldive and Seychelles Islands, establishing colonies or way stations, much as the Polynesians have done with the Pacific in our timeline.

Or possibly not. After all, they've got a whole continent to play with. That may undermine the seagoing tradition. On the other hand, the most effective way to get around the continent is to sail, so that seagoing culture of mariners may thrive.

They might find Madagascar first and colonize it somewhere between 1000 and a few hundred years before the Malay arrive. The Malay arrive at Madagascar to a decidedly different future. It may be that they're wiped out or driven off. Alternately, they may be enslaved or adopted as a subservient culture to the ruling Muans. Its possible that they establish their own population centers and the Muans and Malay divide the island between them in a state of warfare and truce. Or perhaps the Malay merge with the Muans to form a new culture.

If Lemuria exists in this world, then the Muans might find and colonize it. It becomes the third major center of Muan civilization, after Mu and Australia. If not, then they find the Kerguelen and Crozet archipelagos. It's unlikelyl that they occupy them. In our world, those are pretty forsaken lands.

The Muans explorations in increasingly more sophisticated ships and ambitious voyages leads them to discover Antarctica, but they have little use for it.

As an advanced seafaring civilization, they could also discover America, or at least the bottom tip of South America while circumnavigating the Polar region. But apart from establishing an outpost, they find little value, the weather is terrible, the natives are hostile, who needs it.

The ongoing struggle of city states on the Muan continent and its Australian hinterland drives competition and innovation. The northern Muan explorers encounter Asian and Indonesian cultures and obtain the secret of metal and metalworking. Superior technology allows northern Mu to forge temporary Empires. But these fall apart as the technologies spread or are obtained by subjects and rivals. The stalemate goes on.

While geography drives an endless stalemate on the continent of Mu, in the Australian hinterland, the geography is different. The geographical barriers that make conquest so difficult, and worse, that makes conquests so difficult to make stick, are not there. Rather, Australia is a more open country with fewer natural defenses in the forms of ridges, hills and mountains between the city states. One by one, the Australian city states confederate or are conquered, until an Australian empire exists on the west coast which dwarfs the Mu continent city states.

The situation, of course is a repeating one. Carthage grew to overshadow its Phoenician forbears. Macedonia, a provincial hinterland, overwhelmed the warring Greek states. Another hinterland region, Rome grew to encompass the whole of the Mediterranean. Millennia later, Europe is divided into warring competing states, until two hinterland colony states - the United States and Russia grow to a point where they each surpass Europe and divide it between them.

Centers of population and gravity always eventually reassert themselves. Thus the Roman Empire eventually gave way to the Greek Byzantine empire. The Islamic Caliphate eventually gave way to renewed Persian states. In modern times, America's economic domination is giving way to both a European resurgence and a Chinese emergence. So it goes here, power and dominance eventually revert back to the continent of Mu, much like economic and political power shifted from Rome to Constantinople, from the Latin to the Greek.

Then Europe comes along....

I Remember Lemuria

The 19th century was a good time for Lost Continents. Terre Austral was a lost cause by then. But Atlantis was riding high and being taken seriously, and Lemuria and Mu were being discovered.

Lemuria has an almost respectable pedigree. It wasn't driven by racism. It wasn't the work of a crackpot. But at the same time, it wasn't exactly an ancient well-established mythical idea either. In fact, it wasn't very ancient at all.

Lemuria is the invention of a guy named Philip Sclater, a geologist, who came up with it in an article he wrote called "The Mammals of Madagascar" in 1864 in the Quarterly Journal of Science.

What was a geologist doing writing about mammals?

Well, back in that day, scientists tended to be more about SCIENCE than their specialty. Botanists wrote about rocks. Zoologists wrote about plants. And Geologists wrote about mammals. The lines weren't as exact as they are now.

It's like those old 1950's B-movies where the scientist just does SCIENCE stuff, which can involve everything from biology to acoustics to nuclear physics.

Sclater's idea, as set out in his scientific paper, basically wrestled with a peculiar anomaly.

There were lemurs in Madagascar.

No lemurs in Africa, right next door.

No lemurs in the Middle East.

But there were living lemur relatives like lorises and tarsiers, in India and Malaysia.

Somehow, Madagascar had to be connected to India and Malaysia, which were far away... But not with Africa, which was so much closer.

There were more anomalies. The Indian Ocean Islands had giant turtles on several Islands, much like giant turtle fossils found in India. There were overlaps of plants. The people of Madagascar, the Malagasy, seemed more closely related ethnically and linguistically to Malaysia than Africa.

Sclater's answer was that there had to have been a continent or land bridge in the middle of the Indian Ocean that had connected Madagascar to India, allowing species to move back and forth. That continent had obviously sunk.

At that point, his imagination ran dry, because the smartest thing he could think to call the place was Lemuria.... after lemurs. The guy was a wild man, I tell you. I shudder to think about what he might have named his children.

Lemures, by the way, were malignant spirits in Roman folklore. Very scary, very creepy, very supernatural. Lemurs had been named after lemures because of their weird monkey/human/animal features and their strange almost supernatural howls.

But that didnt go through his head at all. No such poetry animated Sclater, he was just thinking ring-tails.

But let's move on for a bit. To get a better understanding of what was going on here with his sunken continent, we have to understand a little of Sclater's world.

You and I live in a world where the continental plates are floating around on a molten mantle, drifting here and there, occasionally whacking up against each other. It stands to reason - any fool can look at a globe and see how Africa and South America fit into each other like puzzle pieces. We can track things backwards to see how it all fit together into a primordial supercontinent. We can even use our satellites to track the slow motion of North America as it moves westward, slowly widening the Atlantic.

The world was different in the 19th century. The continents were not moving around. How could they possibly move? Nope, everything was parked right where it was from the beginning. The giant land masses did not play rousing games of geological bumper cars. South America fitting Africa was just a weird coincidence, among lots of weird geological and biological coincidences. But all these anomalies that didn't mean the continents were in motion. For one thing, the mechanisms and ideas behind plate tectonics simply didn't exist. No one could figure out how continents could possibly move.

Indeed, we see from the rest of the solar system that plate tectonics seems to be comparatively rare. Venus doesn't have them, nor does the Moon or Mars, nor probably Mercury. So it is sort of a fluke. So there was no reason 19th century people should find moving continents credible.

But there was a problem: Clearly species in North America were related to those in Asia and Europe. They had to have gotten from one place to the other somehow. Clearly India and Madagascar both had Lemurs or their cousins and adjacent lands hadn't. There were similar geological formations that seemed related, but were separated by vast distance.

Dawn of Cthulhu – Page 100

So what did they have instead of plate tectonics?

Well, fossil hunters had been finding fossil fish and marine reptile remains far far inland. So it was pretty clear that seas had from time to time covered continents or parts of continents. By tracking fish fossils, you could tell what parts of continents had been underwater and when. It was impossible to go and find land critter fossils underwater, but it stood to reason that if the sea occasionally covered submerged or sunken parts of continents, then it seemed equally reasonable that parts of the sea floor might rise up and amount to Islands and continents.

The obvious answer to the riddle of North America and Asian overlaps was that the two continents must have been joined by a bridge of land, now sunken. Land bridges must have once connected England to Europe. Land bridges must be how kangaroos got from Australia to New Guinea, or how elephants got from India to Borneo.

In fact, land bridges are a real mechanism. They got the England/Europe, North America/Asia bridges right. Panama is a real and current land bridge connecting North and South America. A few million years ago, it didn't exist.

So the theory wasn't actually wrong, it was just incomplete. Basically, science of the day, and for that matter, for a lot of the twentieth century, postulated Earth's history as one of stationary continents and seas which didn't move around like bumper cars, but instead rose up and down like elevators or perhaps like the rising and falling of some leviathan's chest, submerging parts of continents, raising hypothetical new lands.

I have children's science books from the 1960's which say and show this, with elaborate maps showing the distribution of ancient seas and hypothetical lands. There's all sorts of land bridges.

Oh, and for the record, Mountains? That used to be considered shrinkage. You see, the world was hot. We knew that from volcanoes. But it was slowly losing its heat. As heat was lost, the Earth's crust condensed and shriveled, pushing land up as mountains. Think of the Earth as a giant testicle shriveling in the cold. Of course, now we know that Mountains are produced by the motion of continents pushing in one direction, or bashing up against each other.

When I was a kid, I actually had a junior science book that had that explanation. Not testicles, but shrinkage and wrinkling.

Oddly enough, this really did seem to be what happened with Mercury. They've identified physical structures on the planet Mercury that they believe are caused by the planet cooling and the crust shrinking measurably.

It's humbling to realize that even while we were sending men to walk on the surface of the moon, down here on Earth, we still hadn't worked out a clear idea of how our planet worked.

It makes you think about how much we still don't know, and wonder what else we might be mistaken about.

Of course, for a gap like that between Madagascar and India, you needed something more than a bridge. Land bridges are fine for England and Europe, Alaska and Siberia, Malaysian and Sumatra. But Madagascar to India?

A piece of geography that length was likely to be fairly wide, and something that long and wide qualified as a full fledged continent all by itself: Lemuria.

It was just a good idea for its time. It was an inevitable idea for its time, and even if Schlatter hadn't proposed it, someone else would have. The idea was definitely floating around. And perhaps they'd have called it something better. It explained a lot, and it was consistent with the state of knowledge of the era.

The only problem was that it was wrong. But that's hardly a sin. I mean, hell, if I had a nickel for every time I was wrong... Well, I'd have at least ten cents. Maybe a dime.

It was such a good idea that it actually caught on. Lemuria came to be generally accepted by the scientists of Schlatter's day, and subsequent days. There just wasn't a better theory.

But of course, some people can't leave well enough alone. Other theories extended Lemuria into the Pacific, to explain anomalies between Asia and North America... Of course, to get past Australia and Indonesia, our lost continent would have had to have turned into a spaghetti strand at points.

Or possibly, scientists themselves were beginning to confuse Lemuria and Mu.

Lemuria was such a great theory that all too quickly, it started to become a sort of catch all for other little unexplained anomalies.

For instance, why were there no pre-human fossils? Well, obviously, they're all in Lemuria, underwater. Which would make Lemuria the place where the human race originally evolved.

That, ladies and gentlemen, opened the door for the lunatics.

The hypothesis of a lost continent as the birthplace or midwife for the human race was a potent mojo. Lemuria became a potent archetype for all sorts of mystics and visionaries, prophets and fantasy writers.

The most famous of these, was Madame Blavatsky (a real name, or at least, not a joke name), part-time spiritualist, part-time philosopher and full-time, full-bore, raving lunatic. But there was a method to Blavatsky's madness. She proved brilliant at picking up whatever ideas weren't actually bolted to the floor, and morphing them into a bizarre framework of history and mysticism. Atlantis got the treatment of course, and so did Lemuria.

Basically, Blavatsky claimed that humanity had passed through a series of stages or races to reach its present form. These races included sexless egg-shaped energy beings, and four armed giants with eyes in the back of their heads and God knows what else. The idea was that they were constantly degenerating from a spiritual state to ever more degraded and perverted forms of matter, sometimes rising, but always ultimately, falling into decay, to be replaced by a new incarnation.

Lemuria, according to Blavatsky, was occupied by the third root race - hermaphroditic, egg laying giants without intelligence but who were somehow spiritually pure. Some suggest that the third root race might have helped to inspire Edgar Rice Burrough's version of Martians. Purity didn't last.

Blavatsky's Lemurians, without better judgement, got into bestiality. Succumbing to corruption, they died out when Lemuria sank, and a fourth root race rose to take its place over in Atlantis.

Frankly, I don't like to think too much about Blavatsky, since it makes blood run out my ears, and that ruins my shirts. So let's just say that her elevator went to floors in other buildings, her sandwiches were made with unidentified materials, and I'll move along.

Blavatsky was not the only whack-job to take the cautious science and speculation of the day and run it to outrageous dimensions.

Another train of thought which gained unnecessary adherents had surviving Lemurian (human) mystics occupying a hidden sanctuary in Mount Shasta, in California. I assume that Shasta was sort of the vacation home for the Tibetan Lemurians, or something.

Fiction writers used it as fertile ground to mount their own lost race/lost civilization stories. Lemuria appeared in the writings of Robert E. Howard, Howard Philips Lovecraft and Otis Adelbert Kline among many others. It appeared in B-Movie Republic serials, potboilers and adventure thrillers.

One of the most memorable appearances of Lemuria in the world of pulp magazines was the Shaver Mystery. Richard Shaver, was a part time welder, full time schizophrenic (his welding machine talked to him),, and in 1943 he wrote a rambling, somewhat insane letter to Amazing Stories magazine.

The letter was all about robotic dwarfs, Teros, who lived underground and did everything from steal single socks from your washing machine to beaming murderous thoughts in your head. According to Shaver, the Teros were deranged robots left behind by an advanced race of superbeings who had built underground cities.

Ray Palmer, the publisher of Amazing stories edited the letter and published it with the title 'I Remember Lemuria.'

The actual connection to any kind of Lemuria was pretty vague. But Shaver's ramblings caught on and became a controversial obsession for 1950's pulp readers.

Lemuria became a part of pop culture and pulp culture. Basically, when Atlantis was getting too formal and stuffy, you'd drag out Lemuria for that touch of the exotic.

For some reason, Lemurian came to be connected to notions of reptile men, reworked as reptoids in UFO lore and serpent men in pulp fiction.

I guess cute little ring tailed lemurs weren't sinister enough.

As the pulp fiction world attributed ancient civilizations there, and the crazy people parked their delusions in it, the real scientists, who'd started off with a fairly respectable idea, just got quieter and quieter, and started edging out the door.

In the end, plate tectonics made Lemuria unnecessary. The puzzles it was created to solve have all been solved in other ways. So as it turns out, Lemuria was always entirely hypothetical, utterly imaginary. There was never a lost sunken continent in the Indian Ocean...

Except, as it turns out, there actually was...

The Real Lemuria

This next story involves yet another lost continent. Except this one didn't sink, it just sort of evaporated.

The lost continent was Terre Australis (Southern Land). If you go looking at really old maps, you'll see it: An immense rambling land mass occupying the bottom of the map. The great lost continent of the Southern Hemisphere.

Sometimes Australia is a part of Terre Australis. Sometimes the bottom of Africa or South America merges into Terre Australis. It never existed, of course, except in the minds of medieval cartographers and ancient Greek philosophers.

You see, back then, they had this idea of balance. Medieval cartographers began to notice that most of the land seemed to be up in the northern hemisphere; Europe, Siberia, North America, China. Only portions of Africa and South America were in the southern hemisphere. This didn't seem very symmetrical. It seemed downright lopsided.

That didn't make sense. If the world was lopsided, what was to stop the planet from tipping right over? Did that make sense? Well, even if it didn't, they just liked their symmetry.

They just figured that God or Platonic excellence would like things balanced, and that there'd be a big southern continent whose land mass would balance out the north.

They were so confident that it was there they stuck it on maps! Talk about chutzpah. If that wasn't bad enough, several of the maps also feature giant Islands down there which never existed either. I suppose that if you were going to just make up a whole continent for your map, the temptation was to fill it in.

Through the 16th and 17th century, there was nothing to do for it but actually go looking for the damned thing. It didn't go well. Sailors discovered that you could actually sail all the way around the horn of Africa. Later they thought they'd found it, rounding South America, but gosh darn, it turned out that it was only the Falkland Islands or Tierra Del Fueggo.

Captain Cook thought he found it. But it turned out to be New Zealand. He kept looking. Eventually, he sailed all the way around the polar ocean, and somehow, managed to miss finding Antarctica.

He did chart the coast of Australia, but it had already been discovered by the Dutch.

Australia ended up being the geographic consolation prize. It wasn't the Terre Australis that navigators were sure they'd find, defining the shape of the southern hemisphere. That was a much bigger southern continent. Australia was sort of a big-ass island just kind of sitting in the middle of the ocean, like a cork bobbing in a lake. It was named after Terre Australis, but it wasn't actually Terre Australis.

Bit of a let down.

But hope sprang eternal, and as late as the 1770's, the French commissioned an expedition to find Terre Australis, under the leadership of a man named Kerguelen. He found it, or something that he claimed was a lush, beautiful land, just waiting for French colonists. Enthused, the French King sent Kerguelen back with a major expedition.

It was a bad trip. There was a scandal involving an officer who'd snuck a 16 year old girl on board. How do you get away with that on an 18th century sailing ship? There's no room on those things. Eventually, they found it, and everyone was unimpressed.

The new land was merely an island. A fair sized island true, about the size of a New England state. But still just an island. It was rocky and inhospitable, covered with weeds, treeless and barren. It rained constantly, the winds buffeted, the waves were fifteen feet high and the temperatures were near zero. It was the most miserable godforsaken ass-end of a place anyone had ever seen. Kerguelen returned home in disgrace, a victim of his enthusiasm.

Captain Cook visited the place and wanted to call it Desolation, it was so godforsaken. But he decided it should be called Kerguelen instead. Burn!

These early navigators and sailors, they were pricks. You couldn't go out and explore the world and look for new lands to name after yourself, if you weren't a bit of an egotist. They were stiff necked, competitive bastards.

Giving the name back to Kerguelen was a slam. It was 'wow, what a worthless, terrible place you've discovered, I'll make sure its named after you!'

That was pretty much it for Kerguelen. The French found they couldn't do anything with it. They tried sheep, but they all died off. There was some whaling and sealing there for a while. Every now and then a ship would visit for the hell of it.

But the truth was that it is about the remotest place you'd find on the face of the planet. It was as far from land as you'd get. Its isolation and desolation had left it unwanted by humans. Indeed, Kerguelen was one of the last large land masses, short of Antarctica itself, to be discovered. And its one of the only large land masses, again apart from Antarctica itself, never historically colonized by humans. In contrast, places as remote as Easter Island (Rapa Nui) and New Zealand had already been occupied.

Even today, there are more people in Antarctica than Kerguelen, which gives you an idea how godforsaken it is.

There was one thing that should have tipped people off that there was more here than met the eye: Coal was discovered on Kerguelen. That and the remains of forests.

Coal was a signifier. Obviously, any significant amount of coal would have meant that there must have been a much larger land mass. However, the coal was poor quality. It just wasn't worth traveling halfway around the world to mine, when there was better closer. So no one paid much attention to that little signifier.

Then in the last twenty years or so, geological investigations of the surrounding waters turned up layers of volcanic ash and charcoal. Slowly it became clear that the Kerguelen Islands were just the tip of a large structure called the Kerguelen Plateau. This included, as it turned out, the Broken Ridge, another underwater plateau which had been separated by an ocean floor rift.

The Kerguelen Plateau had begun as a volcanic hot spot between 130 and 110 million years ago. Approximately a hundred million years ago, it had risen above the waves as a volcanic mini-continent, sort of like Iceland. Over the next eighty million years, it would rise and sink three times, eventually submerging permanently twenty million years ago. It's now under a mile of water, leaving only few mountain peaks jutting out as islands.

The Kerguelen Plateau was termed a micro-continent, or mini-continent. Estimates vary, but at its maximum, it would have had an area ranging of about half a million square mile. Smaller than Australia, but comparable to Greenland and larger than any of the other continental islands.

Essentially, it's an honest to god, bona fide, genuine sunken continent, albeit a smallish one. For the record, you can check it out on any topographic globe or topographic map of the world's oceans. It's the oblong shape between Africa and Antarctica at 60E and 90E, and 30S and 60S

Currently, the Kerguelen Plateau is located between 45 and 60 degrees latitude. This is approximately the latitudes of Europe from Germany to Norway, or the West coast of North America from Oregon to British Columbia, or New England to Quebec. Bottom line, it could be a pretty European climate, somewhere between France and Finland, but not necessarily harsh, if it was above the water today.

What was this Super-Kerguelen, this lost continent, like? Well, we know from fossil wood, coal and charcoal deposits that it was heavily forested. So its climate would have been much more moderate than it is now. The Indian Ocean is essentially a great circular bowl, extending from the equator to the antarctic, and the water circulates in a gyre, with warm tropical waters moving south, and cold polar waters moving north. As a continental mass, it might have been heated by warm ocean currents, much like the Gulf Stream warms northern Europe.

Of course, remember continental drift. We don't know that the Kerguelen Plateau was always in that spot. It might have been pulled south by the movement of Antarctica to the pole, or shifted by the movement of other continental fragments. In which case, it may have resided in even warmer more hospitable waters. On the other hand, as a volcanic plateau like Iceland, it wouldn't necessarily have been part of the dance of continents. It was a volcanic hotspot originally, like Hawaii or Iceland, it was not originally connected to Australia, or India, or Antarctica.

However, the plateau features sedimentary rocks similar to those found in Australia and India, so it seems likely that it was attached or connected to one or both at some time. But that poses some mysteries for us. Remember, from our discussion of old Lemuria that the continental masses were moving.

At some point a long time ago, all the continents had been smooshed together in an ultimate, mondo, super-continent, Pangea. Over time, Pangea separated into a northern super-continent, Laurasia, which included most of what is now Asia, Europe and North America. The southern super-continent, Gondwana, included most of what became Antarctica, South America, Africa and Australia.

As it turns out, India was part of the original southern super-continent, Gondwana. Africa, India and Madagascar collectively broke away from Gondwana about 165 million years ago. Around 90 million years ago, India/Madagascar broke off from Africa. Then about 60 or 65 million years ago, India and Madagascar broke apart. Madagascar stayed parked relatively close to Africa. On the other hand, India, from about 50 to 55 million years ago, started motoring north, colliding with Asia about 10 million years ago.

Motoring is the right word. So far as we can tell, the Indian plate has moved faster and further than any other known continental plate in Earth's history. No one is sure why. Even now, it's still moving north into Asia at two and a half times the rate that Asia is moving north. It's possible that the India plate is actually shoving Asia north, even as it piles up. It's still an ongoing continental crash, the largest fender bender in history, which is why the Himalayas are so flipping huge (and likely to get bigger).

Australia, on the other hand, seems to have originally been connected to Antarctica, Zealandia and South America, breaking away from the main Gondwana continent earlier than the aforementioned Africa/India/Madagascar group.

This resulted in the southern continents of Australia and South America inheriting the 'slow learners', the more primitive marsupials and monotremes. Australia broke away from Antarctica about 40 million years ago and moved north more slowly.

Antarctica was not originally at the south pole, and was not always glacier covered. Antarctica seems to have started to become ice covered some 30 million years ago, a process that completed only six million years ago. In a sense, Antarctica is another genuine lost continent, this one sunk beneath a sea of ice. It must have had a live population of strange and exotic animals and a diversity of plants. It must have been filled with life, with species and lineages, living out their existences generation after generation. For tens of millions of years, Antarctica was home to a lost world, a land where evolution took strange and unique turns.

For much of its history, the world was warmer down there, and Antarctica, even at or near the South Pole, was ice free. There were even forests and swamps in Antarctica while it was at the south pole, at least for periods of time, and presumably a Marsupial fauna not too wickedly different from Australia.

Antarctica only began to start to get cold after Australia and South America separated from it about 40 and 41 million years ago. Glaciation only appeared about 30 to 35 million years ago. About 23 million years ago, the Drake Passage opened up significantly, separating Antarctica from South America. About 20 million years ago, Kerguelen sank for the final time. By 15 million years ago, Antarctica was fully covered over with an ice cap.

What was happening? Did the world simply get colder?

No. What seems to have been happening was that Antarctica was being kept relatively warm by north/south currents. It was a sort of Gulf Stream effect, the thing that keeps Scandinavia a lot warmer than it ought to be.

So, Antarctica had enough warm that it probably had a reasonable climate. The other continents, Australia, South America, Kerguelen acted as sluices or channel guides, directing cold water north, and guiding warm water south. But when Australia and South America pulled away from each other, years ago, and as Kerguelen sunk, increasingly, Antarctica was surrounded by cold water that simply wasn't going anywhere. The geography that directed warm water south and cold water away was falling apart.

Even worse, as Antarctica became isolated, the cold water increasingly simply tended to circle around Antarctica, becoming the Antarctic Circumpolar Current, which flows 600 times as much water as the entire Amazon, chucking the continent into an extreme deep freeze. It became colder and colder. Colder, in fact, than it would normally have been at the South pole. Literally, we had a sort of refrigerator effect going on.

The last great obstacle to the Antarctic Circumpolar Current was the Kerguelen mini-continent, almost a million square miles of obstinate land, sitting right in the path of the circumpolar current. With Kerguelen there, the current would have broken, being directed north up into the Indian Ocean. This would have resulted in a warm water current being directed south down the other side.

Within five million years of Kerguelen's final sinking, Antarctica had become an ice covered desert. I guess it goes to show you that Earth's polar caps are geological flukes, in a way. There was nothing inevitable about them.

The South Polar Cap exists because there's a continent there to keep the Ice and Snow in place, and a cold circular current to make sure that the cold gets colder. The north polar cap exists because its surrounded by land, which traps the sea ice in place and keeps warm currents from getting in. With different geography, perhaps not markedly different, Earth wouldn't have polar caps at all.

There's something disturbing, when you think about it. Once upon a time, the Antarctic continent was a real place, it had forests and grasslands, prairies and trees. It had lakes and rivers and streams, that fish swam in, with frogs and amphibians. Plants and animals of all sorts lived there, generation upon generation. It was a world to itself, a place with its own history, its own vitality, its own life. Now its gone, all those lineages of millions of generations, tens upon tens of millions of years of history and existence... Ended. Full stop. Deleted. Erased. Buried now beneath miles of ice, beneath an ocean of frozen water.

In a sense, Antarctica is a lost continent itself. A whole world that sank without a trace millions of years before there was a human being to notice.

But anyway, I've gotten away from Lemuria. The point is that Antarctica and India were separate continental plates with distinct histories, from about a hundred million years ago onwards, they were both marching to their own drummers. Kerguelen, if it was connected to anyone as Gondwana broke up may have connected to Madagascar and India and would have shared flora and fauna with them.

Or it could have connected to Antarctica, and borrowed its plants and animals from there. Ultimately, both Antarctica and India had been parts of primeval Gondwana, so the original package of life forms would have been the same. But between Antarctica and India, tens of millions of years of evolution after the fall of the dinosaurs would have gone in different directions, producing very different landscapes.

On the other hand, it seemed to be more a formation than a plate. There may not have been contact, or even land bridges. There might have been interesting indirect connection between Australia, Antarctica and Kerguelen. Some flora and fauna might have been shared, blown by wind, washed up on shores, carried by birds.

The key, of course, is when, for how long and in what way it would have been influenced by other lands. Kerguelen's history begins in the middle of the Jurassic Age, so its likely that the continent was host to Jurassic dinosaurs. But then it submerged twice during its history. Bad luck for the Jurassic dinosaurs. If it was during the Cretaceous when it re-emerged for the first or second time, it may well have been recolonized by Cretaceous dinosaurs...

Possibly lasting until the final submergence, only twenty million years ago. Or possibly not. I think its pretty far fetched that whatever happened on the Kerguelen Plateau, that any dinosaurs survived there past the 65 million year mark. Certainly none survived in India or Madagascar for any period of time.

The really interesting question is when did Kerguelen lose all contact with India or Antarctica? If they were connected during the age of mammals, in the period between 65 and 55 million years ago, then the Kerguelen Plateau would have shared animal species. Depending on how long they were connected and when they separated, Kerguelen might have acquired a legacy of fairly sophisticated mammals who might have gone on to evolve in all sorts of interesting directions. The most intriguing speculation, of course, involves India and

Madagascar. Both places feature lemurs and pro-simians (fossil lemurs in India's case). Which means.

Lemurs.

Lemurs were a very early prosimian, dating back perhaps sixty million years. Madagascar and India had already separated from Africa and had just begun about to separate from its others. Lemurs were a rafting species, that had made the leap from Africa to Madagascar. It's possible that lemur, as a rafting species could have made a further leap from India to Madagascar. We know that prosimians, lemurs cousins, are in India, so either they rafted over or came into India much later when it joined Asia. But it's just possible that primates, lemurs or prosimians could have leapfrogged from Madagascar, to India to Kerguelen.

So that would have given them potentially forty million years of evolution on Kerguelen. Kerguelen would have been two to four times the size of Madagascar, which means that it might have provided unparalleled opportunities for lemurs or prosimians to colonize and radiate even beyond that offered by Madagascar. We might see giants, perhaps near-hominid lemurs. We might have seen marsh dwellers, or even semi-aquatic forms. Others might have evolved as creepy scavengers or dangerous predators. We might have seen creatures worthy of the Roman name 'Lemure.' In which case, Kerguelen would have truly deserved the name Lemuria.

Or we might have seen something equally exotic. Platypus fossils were found in Antarctica and South America as well as Australia. Perhaps Kerguelen's life came from Antarctica, and it was platypus that diverged and evolved into a unique flowering of egg laying mammal species. Perhaps marsupials had a second or third homeland. The answers to what was once there are now 4000 feet beneath the sea.

Of course, we're speculating. If the second last submergence was before 65 million years ago, then its likely that the dinosaurs of Kerguelen would have vanished. It would have been hard for them to have survived the worldwide extinction there anyway. The submergence might have left the mini-continent bare, with no mammals there to start over. Or if the early mammals had been swept clean sometime between 65 and 20 million years ago by submergence, then it's a new ball game, with the plateau too remote from its neighbors to be colonized. It had sunk three times, each time sweeping itself free of life.

Kerguelen could have produced giant birds like Madagascar and New Zealand. Or it might have developed some other strange oddities, as South America and Australia did. It's likely that some very, very interesting life forms were lost when Kerguelen submerged for the final time. At this point, we'll never truly know.

It would be fascinating to contemplate what the Kerguelen plateau, or as I'm going to call it it, Lemuria, might have been if it had lasted into the modern age. I visualize a broad rain forest landscape, something like British Columbia, perhaps European in climate. I'm being generous here, its equally possible that it could have been cold and barren, and even partially glaciated. But that's a lot less fun. We know that there were forests there once. I would like to believe that once upon a time things walked in those forests, that it was not a silent and empty land.

There might have been strange flora and fauna. But its easy to imagine great sloth like creatures, platypus, perhaps a variety of exotic lemurs and gigantic flightless birds. Whatever lived there, it would have been a unique population of plants and animals with tens of millions of years to develop.

Dawn of Cthulhu – Page 118

Would humans have come to it? Unlikely. As I said, Lemuria was incredibly far off the beaten path, its not on any coherent trade route, its located deep in the ocean far from Asia or Africa. It was only discovered by Europeans because they were searching the area for an imaginary continent.

We know that Madagascar, comparatively nearer Africa, was only settled within the last 2000 years, although there are indications coastal Africans may have visited earlier. New Zealand was occupied only 1000 years ago or less.

Many islands in the Atlantic and Indian Oceans were only found and occupied in the last few hundred years. This Lemuria would have been much further away, harder to get to and much more inhospitable to people coming from tropical lands.

Certainly, it was not going to be discovered by the local African cultures which had done coastal and island hopping. This was not the sort of place you reach with dugout canoe or coastal boat. Lemuria was remote enough that been discovered by non-Europeans, it would have been by sophisticated advanced sailors.

Were there any such sophisticated advanced sailors around? The Phoenicians sailed down the African coast (but not, so far as I know, around the horn of Africa), and with a little bad luck, might have made it there. One could almost imagine them being unable to get home and establishing a civilization that the Europeans might stumble over millennia later. But that's an incredible, lottery level, long shot. The other ancient seafarers - the Greeks, the Romans and the Egyptians never even got into the Indian Ocean in any significant way.

There were Asian seafarers - the peoples of Arabia and the Persian Gulf, India, China, even Southeast Asia, but they were primarily coastal huggers. They never found Australia, or even the significant islands of the Indian Ocean, like Mauritius or Reunion. Lemuria was a lot further away.

The Malay might be the best candidate, since they were able to sail all the way from Malaysia to Malaga, one of histories more stunning accomplishments. On the other hand, Madagascar is a lot closer to Africa than Lemuria is to anywhere. As astonishing as the Malay voyage is, it likely involved a lot of coastal hopping.

So it's a long shot that this culture might have made it to Kerguelen. Again, despite making it to Madagascar, they never came close to the large islands in the deeper parts of the Indian Ocean, and showed little enthusiasm for the cold southern ocean.

The Polynesians were brilliant sailors, but confined to the Pacific. So far as we know, they never ventured into the Indian Ocean. So that's an even longer shot.

Its possible that Lemuria being above the water might mean that there were more islands and island chains in the Indian Ocean, and thus more chance of Lemuria being discovered by leapfrogging, island-hopping sailors.

Again, a long shot. Even if it happened, the European or cold climate wouldn't have been suitable for the tropical crops of most potential discoverers. They'd have considered to a worthless and unsuitable land, or if they'd tried to make a go of it, would have been forced to hunting and gathering. Any civilisation founded there would have been utterly isolated and would have had to adapt to radically different conditions than their homeland.

How far would they have gotten? Would they have produced a mass extinction of the local life-forms? Or would they have managed to domesticate some of the lemures and giant birds? Would they have lived in fear of mysterious nocturnal lemure predators and ghouls? Would they have been able to domesticate local plants to recreate agriculture? Would they have built cities? Cut down trees? Mined coal? Farmed the soil? Or reverted to starving hunter-gatherers? Would they have been a super-sized version of Easter Island? Or of Tasmania?

But no matter what, Lemuria was so utterly remote that no pre-modern culture would have found it. The most likely outcome is that it would have lain empty until Europeans showed up on a delusional quest for the hypothetical continent of Terre Australis. Until a much luckier and happier alternate universe version of Captain Kerguelen finally stumbled across a vast forested virgin land with a somewhat vaguely European climate.

In such a case, we could imagine an initial wave of ambitious French colonization. Perhaps a British takeover during the Napoleanic wars. Perhaps a French or mixed French/English version of Australia/New Zealand in the southern Indian Ocean. We might have seen a society of Europeans, joined by Africans, Malay and Hindu's, creating their own strange little world together.

But whatever the case, it would have added a bit of strangeness to the world.

Even knowing that there was once actually a lost continent in the Indian Ocean, call it Lemuria.... Perhaps not the all encompassing explanation for a biological or geological riddle, not the birthplace of humanity, or a touchstone of occultism... But nevertheless a real place that once existed, inhabited by animals that we can barely imagine, not human, but who were as nevertheless as real in their lives and times as we in ours... there's something magical in that thought.

Ultimately, Lemuria probably wasn't important or significant, except to the things that lived there. There was a world there, that lived and died, that piled generation upon generation of life. And then, it ended.

Isn't that enough?

Kumari Kundam, another Lemuria

The Kerguelen Plateau isn't the only great sunken land mass in the Indian Ocean, and Lemuria was not the only fabled lost continent, there.

The Tamil people of India, like other cultures of India, and indeed, like cultures around the world, had legends and folklore about lost lands submerged beneath the sea. When Philip Sclater came up with his idea of Lemuria, Tamil scholars pricked up their ears. They liked the idea of Lemuria, it seemed to mesh with scraps of mythology and folklore from their own culture. They readily adopted the idea of a Lemurian continent as the ancestral homeland of the Tamil people in the 1890's.

Of course, Tamil scholars readily agreed there wasn't a lot of actual evidence for it. But cultural politics got into the mix. The Indian Subcontinent was dominiated by dravidians, hindus and other nationalities. The Tamils were a minority pushed into the south and Sri Lanka. So the notion that they weren't truly part of India, but had come from a noble history of tens of thousands of years, and a lost homeland sank between the waves, became very popular by the 1920's. The Tamils called this lost homeland Kumari Kandam.

Kumari Kandam is kind of interesting. If part of the inspiration for the other fictional lost continents had been to deny non-white peoples agency for their works, here it's turned on its head. Kumari Kandam was the effort of a non-white people to assert its specialness, its uniqueness. Indeed, if they adopted the notion that Lemuria was the birthplace of the human species, they might even have been claiming the ancestry of the human race - that the Tamils were the first humans as well as the first civilization. That's impressive.

To put it politely, however, it's also not true. Not even a little.

But, there is a nearby sunken land mass. This one is called the Mascarene Plateau. It's a boomerang shaped, submerged mass, between Madagascar and India, just north of Madagasacar. It's marked by a handful of Islands, Mauritius, Reunion, the Seychelles, and its found between 30 and 500 feet below the water, rising out of a sea floor 13,000 feet below. Large parts of it may well have been exposed dry land during Ice Ages when sea levels were as much as 400 feet lower.

Unfortunately, it's not terribly large. Total area is about 100,000 square miles, give or take, which would make it half the size of Madagascar or France, or about equivalent to a mid-sized European country. In that sense, it doesn't really qualify as a lost continent. More like a really big misplaced island. I suppose big enough for the Tamils.

The Mascarene Plateau is, however, a genuine continental fragment. The Kerguelen Plateau is basically a supersized volcanic hotspot with pretensions. But the Mascarene Plateau is an actual leftover of continental break up.

It all begins hundreds of million years ago. The continental plates are floating around. Eventually, they accrete into two supercontinents - Larasia in the north, Gondwana in the South. Gondwana included Madagascar, India, Africa, Antarctica, Australia, South American and some place called Zealandia. Starting about 135 million year ago, Gondwana started to slowly break up, when Africa and South America splitting and drifting north. A hundred million years ago, India and Madagascar broke away from Gondwana. About 88 million year ago Madagascar broke off from India and Antarctica, drifting to its present position. India, on the other hand, started to motor, moving north faster than any other continent and eventually striking Asia 35 million year ago in the world's greatest fender bender. The Himalayan mountains are the product of that ongoing collision.

The Mascarene Plateau appears to have been broken off of India roughly sixty million years ago, perhaps as a by-product of the same tectonic forces that ruptured it from Madagascar. The little continental fragment wasn't terribly stable. It sank. But the forces that ruptured it produced intense volcanism, covering it with lava and creating volcanic islands - Mauritius eight million years ago, Reunion six million years ago.

The Mascarene version of Lemuria never had the chance to be a lost world. Between sinking, and being covered with lava, any flora and fauna inherited from India or Madagascar would have been wiped out long go. The new islands created by volcanism were virgin landscapes populated by whatever seeds could wash up on the shore, be blown by wind, or carried in bird's gullets. Tortoises colonized many of these new islands, while some birds settled and became the flightless dodo.

The plateau is close enough to Madagascar that it's possible to imagine some drift from there, perhaps lemurs and giant birds might have made it, back during the Ice Ages when low sea levels exposed these lost lands. It might have been a real land of lemurs. Unfortunately, if it did happen, there would only have been a few tens of thousands of years at most, before most of it disappeared beneath the waves. There would have been little time or opportunity to spread or diversify into unique species and exotic life.

But if places like the Kerguelen Plateau or Zealandia sank twenty million years ago, the Mascarene plateau, or Kumari Kandam, would have existed geologic heartbeats ago, as recently as fifteen or twenty thousand years.

The Kerguelen Plateau was so utterly remote, that had it existed in our time, it would have probably skipped most of human history.

But the Mascarene Plateau, had it existed in the human era would have been a fundamental part of history. The Phoenicians might have stumbled across it, though that's a long shot. The first people to find and settle might well have been the Tamils who had settled the Maldive Islands further north, perhaps establishing a Kumari Kandam. The austronesian Malay who found their way to Madagascar would have certainly found and settled it. The Arabs would certainly have visited.

You would have seen exotic island kingdoms, joined to Africa, Arabia and India by trading networks. The Portugese, the Dutch, the English and French would have each come calling in turn.

Our Kumari Kandam would have added a bit to our world, a bit of strangeness, a bit of the exotic, a bit of magic.

Other Lost Lands

These are not the only lost lands. The Ice Ages were marked by soaking up huge volumes of water in continental ice sheets. During these times, sea levels would drop dozens of feet, exposing parts of Continental Shelves that are now under water. A few of these are worth mentioning.

The Persian Gulf was once an immense river valley leading to the Indian Ocean. There is some speculation that beneath these waters, are the remains of primordial civilizations that gave rise to Sumer. Beneath these waters may be the true origin of human civilization.

Or maybe not, from what we can tell nowadays, civilizetion began with places like Catal Huyuk and Gobeli Tiki in the Turkish highlands and made its way down to Mesopotamia.

Looking north, the Black sea was once dry land, with glacier fed lakes. Eventually, the Mediterranean sea cut a channel through and filled it up with water.

There's a certain amount of speculation that this would have occurred during the human period. Some speculate that perhaps instead of the Persian Gulf, the true original civilization, or at least an early civilization emerged here, and that the flooding of the Black Sea has come down to us in the form of worldwide myths of a universal flood.

But these are simply modern mythologies. Unlike our forbears, we know that these are genuine submerged lands. But until we develop the tools and the will to conduct archeological searches under a hundred feet of water, in thousands of square miles of sea, it will simply remain speculation.

Heading west during the Ice Age low water levels, the British Isles were joined by land to Europe. Under today's north sea were immense rolling plains occupied by roving herds ancient cattle and mammoths. Prehistoric humans followed, hunting them down.

As the waters rose, a fragment of that survived for a time, and became the island of Doggerland, between England and Denmark. Who might have lived there, what they might have done, no one knows.

Travelling east we have Sundaland. Southeast Asia, much of Indonesia and parts of the Phillipines were once all highlands of a much larger sunken land mass. This southern corner of Asia ended up being home to the last gasp of homo erectus, the origin of the hobbit, homo florensis, and the stomping grounds of early humans. Once again, what wonders might lay buried beneath the waves.

Australia, Tasmania and New Guineau were once part of a single larger continent called Sahel, which is why they share some exotic flora and fauna, including Cassowaries, Wallabies, and exotic birds and marsupials unknown to the rest of the world.

There's even a lost sea. Back when India was motoring north, racing to its date with Asia, a small shallow sea was trapped between them, eventually this sea buckled and was pushed up by the crash, contributing to the Himalalayas. Why is this interesting? Well, among other things, it's believed that this lost shallow sea was where the first whales evolved.

In this world we know, there really are sunken continents and sunken lands. Atlantis may have never existed, Terre Australe, Lemuria and Mu were medieval modern fables. But Zealandia, Kerguelen, the Mascarene Plateau, Doggerland, Sundaland and Sahel were once real.

Perhaps in some of these corners of the world, now buried under the waters, species of animals, early hominids, modern peoples and perhaps even early civilizations now all lost to us lived their lives. Out beyond the waves, genuine continents once held alien landscapes of exotic life.

All gone now, a thing I find sad and wondrous, and somehow magical.

PART THREE:
The Mysterious Monsters of Sesame Street

A Game of Let's Pretend

What sort of animals are Muppets? Well, obviously, they're just jumped up sock puppets, constructions of coloured felt with google eyes and hands up their insides. They're the creations of Jim Henson, Frank Oz and their cohorts.

Okay, fine.

But let's pretend.

Let's pretend that the monsters of Sesame Street are real animals.

Real animals are not simple inventions, but rather, they have pasts and futures, as individuals and as a species. They have consistent discernible traits, which allow us to identify where they come from and where they fit on the tree of life. Their traits and anatomy are adaptations to their environment, and these adaptations allow us to understand both that environment and their relationship to that environment.

Of course, Sesame Street has, over the years, had several hundred Muppet characters. Some of whom are explicitly supposed to be humans, or human analogues, and some of which don't really allow for classification.

But there are a quite a few that might stand up to some critical analysis. Most obviously, there's Big Bird, a large flightless avian, and Snuffleupagus, a pygmy mammoth. But there's also a very interesting series of creatures include Grover, Elmo, Oscar, the Cookie Monster and others. Its pretty obvious that Grover and Elmo are the same sort of animal, based on broad resemblance and physical characteristics. But a closer look suggests that Oscar the Grouch, for all his personal idiosyncracies, shares most or all of the traits. Even the Cookie Monster, a massive creature who is a far cry from the delicate Elmo, seems to be related and fundamentally the same sort of creature.

Indeed, a great many of the Sesame Street creatures who are explicitly not 'something else', birds, humans, bugs, aliens, etc., seem to fall into a common mold. They show enough consistency of traits that we could describe them as a species. Let's call them collectively, the 'Sesame Street Monsters.'

We will note that in addition to the narrow set of monsters we're focusing on, there are many outlier creatures. Animal, the wild drummer, for instance, has prominent teeth, unlike most Monsters. Others have floppy ears, or apparent horns, or furless hides, or piglike snouts

These are obviously a second order of creatures, related to the Sesame Monsters, but different. I think that we can explain these as well. But for now, its more useful to focus on what I would consider the 'core group' of Monsters. The outlier creatures might be better understood and explained in terms of appreciating and understanding the main species.

Dawn of Cthulhu – Page 130

So, in those terms, let us begin our journey by examining the Sesame Monsters themselves.

The Anatomy of Sesame Monsters

What are the consistent traits of the Monsters? Well, they're relatively small or mid-sized animals. Adults range from thirty to sixty pounds in weight.

Some individuals, notably Elmo and Grover seem quite thin, others like Oscar the Grouch are heavier and more physically robust, while still others like the Cookie Monster show signs of obesity. I would argue however, that these differences in build represent individual variation, similar to that found in humans, rather than evidence of different types of species.

They're usually covered with wooly fur which extends over the faces, leaving only eyes, nose, and mouth bare. The fur colour varies from individual to individual, but is usually uniform on individuals.

On some, there can be uniquely coloured or thick eyebrows, or scalp tufts, but these are a minority. There's some variation in facial features and contours, for instance, Oscar lacks a prominent furless nose.

There are exceptions. Some have hairless faces, or seem to be furless.

They are tail-less, or at best, have only small vestigial tails. They have round heads with gaping froglike mouths, flat featureless inner mouths and concealed esophagus, and prominent, even protuberant eyes.

The nose seems to be a vestigial muzzle, lozenge shaped, prominent, but featureless. Their teeth do not appear to be strongly in evidence in most individuals, and are either absent or concealed between the lips and the inner mouth pad.

Their shoulders and upper torsos are narrow, but their arms are long and flexible. The legs seem comparatively short. They have only four digits instead of five, one of which is a poorly differentiated thumb.

Behaviorally, they appear to be intelligent, but their intelligence is on the order of small children, or clever primates. They're predominantly left handed, suggesting consistent right-brain hemisphere domination. They are highly, even extraordinarily linguistic.

So, what does this tell us?

Numerous factors suggest an arboreal life style. If their brains are wired anything like hominids or primates, then left handedness/right-brain dominance suggests an emphasis on spatial relationships which are critical for tree dwellers. The comparatively long arms, and the sweeping movement ranges of the arms, up, out and around, suggest tree climbers and branch huggers.

The reduction from five delicate fingers, to four heavier and stronger digits suggest an evolutionary history where having a powerful grip was more important than fine dexterity. In short, their lifestyle would seem to be more along the lines of holding on, hugging tree trunks and branches, and moving carefully and deliberately. This is quite different from the swinging lifestyle of gibbons, and the free climbing of monkeys. What this may resemble most are the 'tree-lifestyles' of sloths, koalas and raccoons. Instead of swift climbers and swingers, they are clamberers.

In contrast to the arms, their legs are shorter and bandy, suggesting adaptation towards tree climbing. When on the ground, they are clumsy bipeds, with short bouncing strides. Clearly, their upper bodies are so oriented towards tree hugging and clambering that they find quadrupedalism awkward.

The large google eyes suggest binocular vision, another indicator of tree dwelling lifestyle. If you're moving from branch to branc, dozens of feet off the ground, the ability to judge distances finely is crucial. However, the large eyes themselves seem to suggest that these are, or were originally, nocturnal creatures. One interesting feature is the diminutive or absent ears on most.

The shape of the mouths, and the apparent small or invisible teeth is suggestive. First, we can rule out carnivores, who require prominent cutting and shearing teeth.

But even herbivores require heavy duty teeth. Chomping and crushing heavy cellulose fibre takes a lot of effort. Elephants, horses, moose and oxen are all chewing on tough grasses and leaves, reducing them to digestible paste. An elephants teeth weigh twenty pounds apiece, and they take a lot of punishment.

The fact that the Monsters for the most part do not have prominent teeth (arguably, some varieties do) suggest that they've got a fairly specialized diet, perhaps soft rain forest leaves, fruits, berries, tender shoots, etc.

The wide froglike mouths suggest that they sometimes, or often, consume in bulk. If they're eating one leaf or berry at a time, well, you don't need a big mouth for that. If you're stuffing food in, then that suggests you're taking mouthfuls at a time. We actually see this 'cramming big mouthfuls' eating behaviour in a number of specimens.

This implies a primary diet of soft leaves or large fruit. The apparent large flat inner mouth suggests a tough but flexible mouth lining and a feeding reflex which swallows big gulps when the mouth closes.

However, in contrast to the small teeth, they appear to have large heavy jaws, implying steady, even rapid chewing. Humans are traditionally the most delicate eaters, practically all our diet is highly pre-processed, so we have comparatively small jaws. Most other primates, even frugivores, tend towards heavier jaws.

We note that among the Sesame Monsters even the juveniles tend to pear shaped bodies. Basically, the standard body shape is large bottoms and narrow shoulders. Again, this implies a digestive process that emphasizes or allows for volume, and perhaps a long bowel system for food processing. Again, this points to soft leaves as a large component of diet.

Gorillas are generally leafy green eaters, but there's not much food value in that stuff, so they have to eat a lot of it. Which means that they've both got to spend a lot of time eating, and they've got to have pretty full stomachs for comparatively paltry returns. Gorillas are prone to being pot bellied for this reason, much like the Sesame Monsters.

On the other hand, chimps are much more strongly frugivores (fruit eaters). It's a highly specialized, but much more high energy diet, so the chimps don't need to eat as much. They get a bigger bang for their buck... so no pot-bellied chimps. Again, the Monsters physical morphology suggests that their lifestyles are tending to resemble sloths or koalas, or even pandas.

On the other hand, the behaviour of the Monsters seems more energetic than sloths, koalas or even pandas. They're outgoing, curious and even inclined to seek out high value foods like cookies. This suggests that while their adaptations allow a 'soft-leaf' diet, their tastes are considerably more diverse. Unlike koalas and pandas, they probably are not restricted to a single brand of plant, but might take advantage of a variety of food sources, different fruits, berries, different sorts of bamboo shoots or leaf sprouts.

The wooly fur suggests both high humidity and wide temperature ranges. They're rain forest creatures, but sometimes it gets cold.

What are they?

First things first, they're obviously primates.

But what kind?

Taxonomically, we can broadly look to four categories of primates: Hominids, apes, monkeys and prosimians.

To start, we can pretty much rule out hominids. Homo florensis aside, there's nothing in the hominid line that would lead to anything like them. There are a number of divergences, the wide mouth and heavy jaw, the absence of forehead, the prominent eyes, the fur covered face, all of which suggest that they're not hominids, or if they are, they're a pretty radical branch off the family tree.

Apes? Well, like Apes and Hominids, the Sesame Monsters are tail-less. But its pretty clear that the gap between the Monsters and Great Apes is as big as that between the Monsters and Hominids. Still, there is arguably a resemblance between the lesser apes, the Gibbons, and the Monsters. On the other hand, the Monsters don't seem as highly adapted as the Gibbons to a tree swinging lifestyle...

Or more accurately, they're differently adapted. The two species have taken different paths. This is an important consideration. A particular lifestyle or evolutionary pathway demands specialized adaptations. Try to change the lifestyle, and those adaptations become handicaps. Evolutionarily, an animal would literally have to evolve backwards, retracing its steps to a more generalized form, and then proceeding forward down a different lifestyle fork. That's hard to do, particularly when the more generalized forms are still around and competing. Thus, highly specialized animals tend to either remain as they are, or become even more highly specialized in the directions that they're already going.

What this means is that gibbons are already highly specialized for a particular kind of lifestyle. They're committed to their path. It would not be easy for them to evolve radically in a different but similar lifestyle.

A gibbon that went down the sort of pathway that produced the Sesame Monsters, would only produce a slightly different kind of gibbon.

The best we can say is that gibbons and Sesame Monsters had a common ancestor whose offspring went off in two different directions and made different commitments and trade offs in their lifestyles. The same goes for the great apes and hominids.

I'll also leave out monkeys for the same reason. The Sesame Monsters are tree huggers rather than nimble tree climbers like monkeys. On the ground, monkeys are fully quadrupedal, not poorly bipedal. It's possible that some line of monkey went down the sloth/koala road, but there's no clear precedents. Besides which, monkeys, as well as apes and hominids are diurnal (day) creatures, and their faces are furless.

Again, the Sesame Monsters seem to be a parallel line to monkeys, not an offshoot of them. So we have to look further back for a common ancestor.

So what's left? Prosimians. This is the original primate line that gave rise to old and new world monkeys, apes, hominids. Modern prosimians include the Lemurs of Madagascar, and the tarsiers of Asia, lorises, pottos and galagos of Asia's and Africa's rain forests.

A number of the prosimian characteristics seem to match up with the monsters. Their faces, like the Sesame Monsters, are fur covered, rather than naked like other primates. As a group, they tend to be nocturnal with large eyes. Several of them, notably the lorises, pottos and tarsiers have round heads and flat faces, with small ears. The lorises and pottos are notably tail-less or stump-tailed, and are slow moving clamberers. Some of the extinct lines of lemurs evolved specialized lifestyles similar to sloths and koalas.

So, did the Sesame Monsters evolve from those lemurs? Nope. The lemurs of Madagascar went off in their own direction. But they're close enough to a starting point, to a common ancestor, that some of their representatives embraced similar lifestyles.

In fact, the best and closest analogue to the Sesame Monsters are the lorises and pottos. Here is a typical description, snagged from wikipedia:

"Lorises have a close, woolly fur which is usually grey or brown colored, darker on the top side. The eyes are large and face forward. The ears are small and often partly hidden in the fur. The thumbs are opposable and the index finger is short. Their tails are short or are missing completely. They grow to a length of 17 to 40 cm and a weight of between 0.3

and 2 kg, depending on the species. Lorids are diurnal and arboreal. Unlike the closely related galagos, they have slow, deliberate movements and never jump. With their strong hands they clasp at the branches and cannot be removed without significant force."

Note the wooly fur, the round heads, large forward facing eyes, the short or missing tails, the reducing finger, slow deliberate movements and strong grip. There's more than a passing resemblance. This is probably the starting point of the Sesame Monsters.

Did the Sesame Monsters evolve from lorises? Nope, not quite. For one thing, lorises are a specialized species on their own, they're clearly smaller, and opportunistic insectivores and predators. But clearly, modern lorises are closely related to the Sesame Monsters.

So, we can safely assume that they belong to the same family, Lorisidae, and spring from a common, ancestor which was probably quite loris-like, which may have also been an ancestor for lemurs, mew world monkeys, old world monkeys, apes and hominids. In short, they represent a sixth major line of primates.

Now, lorises themselves, along with other prosimians like the pottos, tarsiers, galagos etc. are pretty much losers in the evolutionary sweepstakes. Sure, they've managed to hang on in isolated and specialized niches. For the most part, though, they've been pretty thoroughly crowded out by their more advanced and aggressive cousins, the monkeys and apes.

Indeed, the only other place where the prosimians really came into their own was in Madagascar, where the lemurs, without competition, had an evolutionary flowering, producing dozens of species and occupying niches of monkeys, woodpeckers, sloths and apes.

Interestingly, if we look to the closest evolutionary analogues to the Sesame Monsters, the sloths, koalas and mega-lemurs, we find that both of these evolved on island continents which were outside the big mainstream of evolution.

This suggests that the Sesame Monsters in order to have evolved as far and become as sophisticated and specialized as they have, were probably an island species. Out on the mainland, their slow deliberate lifestyles could never have competed with their agile cousins. In short, they needed their own Madagascar, a fair sized island of rain forests, which would be hospitable to a large specialized population of relatively big primates.

The Anatomy of Great Big Birds

In contrast to the Sesame Monsters, who were tricky to analyze, Big Bird at first seems pretty straightforward. He's just a giant flightless bird. No problem.

There are a lot of examples of big flightless birds: There are the moas of New Zealand and the elephant birds of Madagascar, both recently extinct; Australia produces cassowarys and emus, and even bigger extinct forms; South America has a rhea; Africa has the ostrich; Antarctica has Penguins: Ancient South America produced the giant diatrama flightless predator birds; while Ancient North America produced the giant phororacos flightless predator birds; Mauritius produced the dodos and Hawaii produced (also recently extinguished) lines of flightless geese.

So there's ample precedent for big-ass flightless birds, including several that make Big Bird look tiny, and a few that are downright scary.

From this rich sample, we can draw a few conclusions that will apply to Big Bird. First, with the possible exception of the sstrich, all the giant flightless birds occur on islands or island continents. Australia, of course, is an Island continent. South America was, for much of its post-dinosaur history, an isolated Island continent. Even North America, during the age of its giant predator bird, was an Island continent (though it quickly joined up with land bridges to Asia). The ostrich may have originated in India, back when it was an island continent before it merged with Asia. Madagascar and New Zealand have always been islands since before the dinosaurs ended. Hawaii and Mauritius are volcanic islands which were never connected to any mainland.

For the record, Mauritius was an Island of about 2000 square kilometers, and produced the dodo, about 3 feet tall, and fifty pounds weight. The big island of Hawaii is about 10,000 square kilometers and produced its flightless geese. For the real monsters, you needed islands the size of Madagascar (590,000 square kilometers), New Zealand (270,000 square kilometers), or island continents of millions of square kilometers.

The reality is that flight is a bird's major advantage to escaping from predators. This means that they have to be small enough to fly and escape easily. Geese have an advantage in that they occupy an environment where its hard for predators to get at them. This allows them to grow larger. In order for birds to grow large enough that they get too heavy to fly, their environment has to be free from predation.

To get really big, the ecological niches have to be free, or at least, not fully occupied by competing big mammals.

So Big Bird, like his brothers in feather, evolved on an island. And it must have been a fair sized Island. We have a range: Obviously, places like Hawaii and Mauritius are too small, they never produced much larger than turkey sized specimens. Places like New Zealand and Madagascar produced giants that dwarfed even Big Bird. So, Big Bird's Island had to have been reasonably hefty, smaller than New Zealand, bigger than Hawaii. Perhaps something in the neighborhood of Sri Lanka or Hispaniola.

And of course, it would have to have been an island which hadn't been connected to the mainland for most of the last fifty or sixty million years. Specifically, it had to be separate long enough for something like Big Bird to have the room and time to evolve.

Has it always been that isolated? That's an interesting question, and we'll return to it later.

Now, let's look a little more closely at Big Bird. What do we notice?

Thick legs. Thick legs and big, flat, wide feet. That's interesting. If we look at the other modern giant birds, the ostrich, rhea, cassowary, emu, they've all got long skinny legs, and narrow feet.

There are reasons for that. Basically, long or spread out feet give better traction, but there's a drawback, too many moving parts, too much drag. Think about it: You're racing along at a clip of forty kilometers an hour, that's a lot of footfalls, and that's a lot of force being applied to the ground. The last thing you want to do is to break some toes, and the more toes you are putting down, the more foot surface, the more risk.

So critters that are built for speed tend to reduce their 'footprint.' Dogs and big cats literally are walking on their fingertips, with dainty tiny paws. Hoofed herbivores reduce their footprint to only a couple of toes, dispensing with the rest. The horse is down to one toe. Ostriches do most of their running on two toes, while the other giant birds are three toes, but go with slender narrow toes. Most of the running power is in the upper thighs, so you get dainty slender legs, over and over again.

So a creature with broad, thick feet probably is not a fast runner by inclination. It may be trading off speed for traction. Sand or snow runners, marsh dwellers, etc., tend to have broader feet.

As for thick legs, there's two things that get you thick legs. One is carrying a lot of weight. Elephants, Rhinos, Hippos, Brontos etc. Big Bird stands over eight feet tall, and probably weighs in somewhere between 200 and 400 pounds. The Elephant Birds of Madagascar who may have gone three or four times Big Birds weight had heavy legs, though not as heavy as Big Birds seemed to be. The biggest Moas stood twice Big Birds height, but had thinner legs.

So, what does this suggest? Well, dwarf elephants and hippos inherit thick legs, not because their current weight needs them, but they have the leftover body plans of much bigger animals. So its possible that Big Bird's particular species is a dwarf form, and that the full sized editions were much, much bigger. Like maybe twenty feet tall? Jurassic Park here we come.

But then, in order to support a species that big, you might need an island Madagascar sized or better, perhaps even an island continent. Doesn't seem likely.

So what's the other possibility? Muscular legs are required for heavy or complicated traction issues and unstable ground. Humans have thick legs because we started off as tree dwellers, our evolutionary history emphasized lots of ranges of movement.

Complicated ranges of movement in awkward ways, over simple fast nimble running, tends to require thicker bones and a lot more muscle and tendons all the way through. In fact, humans are not built for running at all, take a look at our feet, at best, we've made some compromises by shortening the toes, but its still a slow-walking foot. Our legs are built for a lot of different movement.

There was one species of moa, mid-sized, perhaps about five feet tall, that was known for having legs as thick and heavy as Big Birds. This appears to have been a marsh-dwelling, wading bird. It needed heavy muscular legs and big flat feet because it had to trudge around in muck. This would seem to be Big Bird's evolutionary choice, our giant yellow friend is a marsh and swamp wader. He's not a runner, he's a mud slogger.

Nor is that the end for Big Bird. Let's take a look at the other end. Unlike many birds, Big Bird's eyes are set together and facing forward. This means strong binocular vision, weak peripheral vision. Most birds eyes are set off to the sides of their head to maximize peripheral vision.

After all, when you're a bird, you're usually pretty small, your defense mechanism is a fast escape, and so you want to see anything sneaking up on you. Meanwhile, most of the stuff you are eating, be it seeds, grain, berries, etc., doesn't require a lot of complicated visual acuity, in that you need to pinpoint it precisely. It's usually not moving around, its going to be there when you get there, and there's usually more of same laying around in the vicinity of the first one. So birds generally emphasize peripheral vision, the widest possible range gives not only warnings of predators, but a pretty good idea of what food is in the local neighborhood.

Fairly few birds set their eyes forward. Eagles, Hawks and most dramatically, Owls. These birds are not worried about predators because they are predators. And the economics of their lifestyle are different. Basically, their environment is a lot more empty of food than a seed eating bird. Think about it. Seeds don't fall one at a time. So a place that contains a tasty seed is likely to contain a whole bunch of them. You fly in, poke around, eat your fill.

On the other hand, prey behaves differently. If you're hunting mice, you aren't going to get a whole bunch of mice hanging around out in the open. You're looking for a single mouse. That mouse doesn't want to be caught, so its taking evasive action, or hiding, or moving. And when the warning comes, all the other mice hide even harder. So vision adapts to spot, zero in on, and accurately zoom down on that one mouse. You don't need peripheral vision, because all the rest of the mice are going to be making themselves scarce.

Big Bird's eyes are very strongly binocular, as we've said. And more than that, they're extremely large, even for his size. Which suggests that Big Bird is strongly processing a lot of complex and subtle visual information. Indeed, the size of the eyes suggest that Big Bird's ancestors may well have been nocturnal.

Does Big Bird's sophisticated binocular vision, similar to Owls mean that our big yellow friend is a predator? Nope. The beak is all wrong. Predator birds have relatively short, powerful, sheering beaks. Look at eagles or owls. Even look at crows. Beaks tell a lot about lifestyle. Woodpeckers have heavy, reinforced beaks for pounding or digging through bark. Flamingos have these 'roman nose' beaks that they use for filter feeding, turning their heads upside down and dragging through water. Parrots have powerful hooked bills for cracking nuts and peeling fruit. Ducks have flat beaks for rooting through muck.

In Big Bird's case, the thick legs and wide feet suggest a slower walking rather than running lifestyle, that is not consistent with a predator. But on top of that, he doesn't have a predators beak. It's safe to leave the kids around him.

So what does that beak tell us about Big Bird's lifestyle? Take a look at it. It's long. Long beaks are significant. An animal doesn't have a beak longer or stronger or sharper than it needs. Big Bird's bill is long in absolute terms, but comparable to the size of his head. It is rounded, not blunt or sharp. It doesn't look particularly heavy, which means that in terms of the potential muscle supporting it, its not particularly strong. A really strong sheering beak would be a lot heavier and more massive.

So, what is it not? Well, its not a nutcracker. It's not a woodpecker. It's not a scavenger beak. Or a predator bill. If he was a grass eater, or grazer, like a horse, you'd expect a short wide bill for taking up mouthfuls of grass, something heavy with powerful muscles for shearing and tearing grass over and over.

Nope, this is a beak built for poking your nose into things, but not hard or tough things. Big Bird's diet consists of relatively small, relatively soft objects, which it has to 'fish' for. So what's Big Bird actually eating? Well, to start with, possibly frogs and salamanders, snails, slugs, big tasty insects, small marsh or river fish, berries, fruit, soft tender plant shoots or leaf buds. Big Bird is moving relatively slowly through a complicated, visually dense environment. So my guess is that he is an omnivorous opportunist, feeding widely upon a wide range of special materials. Not unlike humans.

There are different feeding strategies. One is to just consume whatever is readily available, like grass. That's usually low value, though plentiful, so the strategy is to consume a vast amount of it. You can get pretty big that way, as elephants, horses and oxen show us. Or you can be a very specialized feeder upon high value but less common food. Which is the strategy of creatures from hummingbirds to blue whales. You can get pretty big that way, orang-utan are exclusively fruit eaters and they're hefty tree dwellers. The thing is that you have to be very good at finding and eating your specialized food. Usually that means highly adapted.

Big Bird has chosen the second route, he's a specialized eater, and probably he's got a series of specialties. In evolutionary terms, Big Bird is probably the closest thing birds have ever produced to hominids.

And he's smart too. More on that later.

Before we leave Big Bird, we'll take note of one last anatomical peculiarity: The adaptation of his wings. Big Bird's wings have devolved, or re-evolved back into reasonably functional arms and hands.

Impossible? No. While its true that for most flightless birds, the wings become useless appendages, fast runners still use them for balance, and ostriches use them for sexual display. The wings have lost their original function, but remain available for other functions. In fact, with the phororacid giant killer birds of North America, their wings may have re-evolved into clawed or taloned gripping limbs, increasing their resemblance to their cousins, the T-Rexes. Another

South American bird, the quetzalcoatl, while a young flightless chick, has clawed wings which it uses to climb with. When it matures, its wings develop more normally and it loses the claws. So its entirely possible for Big Bird's species to adapt its wings into functional limbs.

What sort of adaptation do we see? Big Birds wings/arms are relatively short. They can't reach up over its head, or down to its toes. At least, they can't without ducking his head or bending at the knee. There do not appear to be claws or talons, or even apparent fingernails. There's some indication of differentiation into fingers. There may or may not be a crude thumb. Big Bird doesn't display fine dexterity. The wings are the same colour and have the same feather texture as the rest of the body, so they aren't used for sexual display. Or probably not for sexual display: We're generalizing from a single possibly not fully mature example to both sexes of an entire species, so we can't be sure.

So what are Big Bird's wing/arms for? Why did they develop? In terms of development, I can see two possible functions that might have conferred evolutionary advantages and been easily reachable. The first is sex.

Shocked?

But let's be serious here. These are gigantic, slow moving, two legged creatures trying to mate. They're inhabiting a tricky, possibly messy landscape of swamps and marshes, so probably there's an advantage to being able to mate standing up. Standing mating is tricky. It helps if you are able to hold onto your partner. Even a minimal grip is helpful. Otherwise you're pretty much reduced to running at your partner and hoping one thing goes into another. A rousing game of bumper cars might be fun, but its not the best way to produce eggs.

A 'mating grip' or 'mating hug' would be within the original movement ranges of the wings, and as I've noted even a minimal grip would be helpful. Even some large modern birds who mate on the ground, such as geese or eagles are known to 'cover' their mates with their wings, as a sort of primitive mating grip. So there's both an advantage and the basic elements already in place to develop it. Big Bird's 'arms' probably began from using wings for a mating grip or cover.

The other thing? Grooming. Consider the Big Bird's environment. Swamps and marshlands, brush, early stage rain forests (where the trees and fruit aren't too high). That's a landscape loaded with insects, parasites, debris, dirt, and whatnot. So grooming is going to be a major priority. Big Bird's wings, if they evolved increasing movement ranges for mating hugs, would have an incentive to adapt further, to become more flexible in reaching its own body. Grooming adaptations might develop digit differentiation, fingers or fingerlike structures. Indeed, grooming might be so important that it may be a key portion of Big Bird social activities among their own species.

Of course, as a structure becomes more sophisticated, it can take on new functions. Long digits and a gripping thumb was critical to hanging onto tree limbs. But once you've got a working hand, you can do all sorts of cool things with them.

In this case, if you are developing arms from wings, then you can start to carry things. Things like nesting materials, particularly if the beak is comparatively weak for that purpose. Things like eggs.

This might be pretty critical for the Big Birds. After all, look at their environment. It's hardly stable and sanitary. Who wants to lay eggs in a swamp?

Worse, the Big Birds are very big animals with narrow diets. So they can't stay in one place too long or they 'mine out' the local food sources. There are ways around that. Penguins stock up on food, get really fat, trek miles inland and spend months starving and balancing eggs on their feet so that they'll hatch in a safe place. Another approach is for the mommy bird to stay with the eggs, and the daddy bird, or other birds of the social unit, to forage widely for food for her.

But another approach might be for the Big Birds to be able to pick up the eggs, tuck them under the arm, and carry them to safer neighborhoods from time to time. This would be a major advantage over other birds, who are pretty much stuck with their eggs where they laid them. Indeed, this is the principal vulnerability of birds, their eggs. So an adapted ability to pick up and carry eggs, either as a safety measure or a lifestyle, is a major advantage. It's probably also not a bad thing for the hatchlings, either.

As to whether or how systematically they may have carried other items, that's difficult to say. Big Bird on Sesame Street has constructed a large complicated nest, and furnished that nest with large objects, including a bubble gum dispenser, a clock with no hands, a feather duster, a football helmet, a golf bag with one club, a hurricane lamp, a megaphone, a picture of Mr. Hooper, a Roman bust, a tricycle wheel, a watering can, an old record player, an umbrella, a mailbox, and a pair of snowshoes. Presumably, some or many of these objects could not have easily been carried in a beak, and would have been carried by arms.

Big Bird is occasionally seen carrying objects, including suitcases, and quite often a teddy bear. The teddy bear, named Riley, suggests that we are watching biologically determined

displacement behaviour. Because Big Bird likes to carry
around his love object, his 'bird-thromorphized' teddy bear,
its likely that Big Birds in the wild frequently carried their
eggs and hatchlings.

Big Bird's arms and hands are a perfect example of the
mechanism of adaptation. Originally useful for flight, after
that function was lost, they found a secondary use in mating.
Adaptations which enhanced that function allowed the Big
Birds to develop 'function creep' as the increasingly strong
and flexible gripping wings began to be used for grooming
and then other purposes.

As for other, more intangible qualities, it is linguistic, yes.
Intelligent, definitely. Social, almost certainly. But without
seeing more of the Big Birds, or seeing them in the wild, we
can make few generalizations. Were they tool users? There's
little evidence of that from the one specimen that we see. Big
Bird seems an indifferent tool user, most of which he derives
from the humans around him. Is tool using part of their
repertoire in the wild? We can't say.

How social were they? Did they travel in herds or flocks,
troops, extended family groups, or were they solitary
creatures? Again, we don't know. From the behaviour of the
one specimen, we see that while fairly independent, he bonds
socially with humans and these bonds are very important. So
we can assume that the Big Birds were not necessarily solitary.
On the other hand, it would probably be difficult for
creatures that big with diets so particular to support large
populations, so most times, Big Bird's probably moved in
small families or troops.

And that's about as far as we can take Big Bird for the
moment. So let us take a moment to contemplate the Big
Birds in their natural setting, proud and stately giants,

meandering slowly but carefully through the swamps and borderland rain forests of their home, moving in small family groups, with eggs or hatchlings tucked under their wings, their gazes continually searching their landscape for food or items of interest. And let's move on.

The Anatomy of Snuffleupagus

Like Big Bird, Snuffleupagus is a deceptively simple creature. What is he? Well, obviously, he's from the elephant family. The trunk and heavy tree-trunk limbs are dead giveaways. Snuffleupagus shaggy fur, small ears and sloping back suggest that he's derived from the Mammoth line, which emerged some six million years ago, and became extinct in the last ten thousand years.

The most likely ancestor is the Southern Mammoth, which evolved from the African Mammoth and spread into Europe and Asia approximately four million years ago. Seven hundred thousand years ago, as the ice age hit, the Southern Mammoth gave way to the Steppe Mammoth and then to the Wooly Mammoth. So we can identify Snuffleupagus ancestry as dating back one to four million years, when he diverged from the Southern Mammoths.

Dwarf Elephants and Mammoths are not uncommon in history. Indeed, there was a species of dwarf Mammoth that survived on Wrangel Island off of Alaska until about 1,500 B.C., and which seems to have been not much larger than Snuffleupagus. On the Island of Cypress, up until 11,000 years ago, in the Mediterranean, there was a dwarf elephant whose weight was only about 440 pounds, pretty hefty, but a far cry from ancestors who reached 25,000 lbs. Dwarf elephants or Mammoths have also been described on the

Islands of Sardinia and Sicily, in Malta, Crete, on the Dodecanese and Cyclades Island groups in Greece, on Channel Islands in California, and on the Flores and Sulawesi Islands in Indonesia, with some of the dwarfs being a mere four feet at the shoulder. So Paleontology gives us a great many dwarf cousins about the same general size as Snuffleupagus.

But these precedents tell us something very important about Snuffy. You see, dwarf pachyderms are exclusively island creatures.

Biologically, this makes sense. An elephant is a lot of biomass. On open ranges with an unlimited food supply, its to their advantage to be as big as they can get. Put them on an island with a limited food supply, and the equation changes. They start to evolve smaller and smaller, in order to sustain more individuals, on the same food supply.

That's the quirky thing about Island ecologies. Large animals trapped on Islands will tend to get smaller in response to the more confined ecosystem. Indeed, it happens locally. A Natural Resources officer once revealed to me that the moose on Hecla Island in Lake Winnipeg tended to be slightly smaller, statistically, than the moose on the mainland. So, we get pygmy elephants and mammoths everywhere, pygmy hippos on Madagascar, pygmy deer on the Jersey Islands, etc.

Interestingly, small animals on islands can get larger and grow into comparative giants without competition or predators. Thus, the moas and elephant birds of Madagascar and New Zealand. The forty pound pigeons we called dodo birds. The giant tortoises and iguanas of Galapagos, and so forth.

Now, the interesting thing here, is that we can get an idea of the island size ranges that you need to produce a

Snuffleupagus. Places like Sri Lanka (25,000 square kilometers), Sumatra (470,000), Java (126,000) and Borneo (280,000) have full sized Indian elephants. They're well watered tropical islands large enough that there's no pressure to produce dwarves.

On the other hand, you get Dwarves on Crete (8,400), Cypress (9,200), Sicily (25,000) and Sardinia (24,000), Wrangel (7300), Flores (14,000), Sulawesi (174,000).

Sulawesi (Celebes) is the largest Island producing pygmy pachyderms, but if you look at a map, it's a very strange Island made up of all these long narrow lobes. So perhaps geographically it divides up much smaller than its apparent surface area. As the outlier, I think we can justify throwing it out.

Now of these, Sri Lanka is the smallest island that has full sized elephants, and its comparable in size to Sicily and Sardinia. We can assume that its rain forest climate is more hospitable to Elephants than the Mediterranean climates of the Italian islands. It would have been warmer and rainier in ancient times of course, but perhaps less than Sri Lanka now. Sri Lanka, Sicily and Sardinia probably sit at the absolute thresholds of full size and pygmies, where you can tip either way, depending on the climate, geography, food supply.

If we adjust for climate and rainfall, we might estimate that Sri Lanka is 15% more fertile for elephants than ancient Sicily and Sardinia. Which suggests that in the tropics, the threshold size where you'd start to get pygmies is probably around 20,000 to 25,000 square kilometers. If Sri Lanka was at Mediterranean latitudes, it might need to be 36,000 square kilometers to have a viable full sized population.

Viable populations of pygmies show up on Islands between 10,000 and 7,000 square kilometers. Wrangel, in the arctic ocean off of Siberia must be pretty sparse and empty, though again, we make allowances for a warm period. So presumably, you might have a successful breeding population on smaller Islands which were much warmer and richer. Let's guess that 3000 square kilometers is the lower limit.

Pygmy elephants also show up on California and Greek islands of only a few dozen or few hundred square kilometers. But I don't know that these would be viable breeding populations, and these islands are probably the remains of much larger islands mostly submerged by sea levels. So I'll ignore them.

On the whole, Snuffleupagus home island, assuming that its in the tropics, is probably somewhere between 20,000 and 3000 square kilometers in area. Do I have an Island in mind? Nope, I'm just trying to work backwards from Snuffy to his environment.

Downsizing seems to take place quickly. The Wrangel Island mammoths were separated from the mainland 12,000 years ago, and were at pony size 3000 years ago. So they downsized in only about 9,000 years or less. The Channel Island mammoths developed about 40,000 years ago.

One key feature of Snuffy's Island is that it must have either been connected to the mainland, or it must have been so close that the elephants or mammoths would have survived a swim. By and large, elephants are not well noted swimmers. Push come to shove, they can float for a bit. But beyond a mile or so, forget it.

Now, here's an interesting thought. With the Sesame Monsters, the Big Birds and the Snuffleupagus, we keep coming back over and over to the fact that each of these must have evolved as island creatures. They couldn't have evolved on the mainland.

So.... Same island?

The Fabled Island of the Talking Animals

New York is a long way from the island, or islands where the Sesame Street Monsters and their colleagues must have originally evolved.

Was it one Island? Or two? Or three? We can't say for sure. It's highly likely that the Sesame Monsters and the Big Birds are from the same Island and probably evolved at the same time. For now, let's call this Sesame Island.

The Birds and Monsters both seem to be creatures of similar backgrounds, probably temperate or tropical rain forest types. Certainly we know that lemurs and elephant birds both evolved in Madagascar, so there's proof that they do get along.

And they would both need similar long periods of isolation on the order of fifty million years or better. Simply put, if the mainland life was able to get onto the island, then predators and competitors would have prevented giant birds or advanced sloth-like prosimians from ever evolving.

But this poses a problem, because in evolutionary terms, Snuffleupagus is a johnny-come-lately. His ancestral species, the southern mammoth only goes back some four million years and died off about a million years ago. So the Snuffleupagus emerges far more recently. If it's the same Island, how does he get there? And what does it mean?

Dawn of Cthulhu – Page 155

The key lies in the Ice Ages starting about three million years ago. The Ice Ages soaked up lots of water and locked it up as ice. Sea levels dropped dramatically. As a result, Australia and New Guinea were connected as a single land mass. Most of the big islands of Indonesia were connected to Indochina and the Asian mainland. Sri Lanka was part of India. The British Isles were a part of a greater European land mass. Land bridges joined Asia to North America.

And of course, there's tectonic plates, moving against each other. Pushing up crust or letting it sink down, even creating its own temporary land bridges in the form of chains of islands or mountainous ridges.

So, on our hypothetical Sesame Island we can postulate a long period of isolation from the mainland, perhaps dating all the way back to the end of the age of dinosaurs.

The inhabitants of this Island cannot walk there. They either fly there, as the birds did. Or they're castaways, small prosimians clinging to trees washed away by floods or tsunamis. The lemurs of Madagascar and the new world monkeys of South America both arrived on their shores as castaways. Indeed, we can speculate about a few of the other animals that would have wound up populating Sesame.

Lizards and turtles, as we've seen with Indian Ocean tortoises and Galapagos tortoises and iguanas. Perhaps a few other tree clingers, small insectivores or leaf eaters. By water, some of the better swimmers, crocodiles and otters perhaps might make it.

The period of initial colonization, as we've noted, would have been about forty to fifty million years ago. Our yardstick is the period when the prosimians were at their height. After that, they were in decline and monkeys and later apes were taking over.

To produce the giant birds and advanced prosimians, our Island would probably have to have been about the same ballpark as Sri Lanka, give or take. Say about 25,000 to 15,000 square kilometers.

And it's probably situated in the tropics, probably in the rain corridor. Our reconstruction of the Sesame Monsters puts them as rain forest creatures, and our analysis of the Big Birds also places them as swampy creatures. This means that the island has to be wet and humid, though there may be a cold season, most likely from Antarctic currents.

It's likely that Sesame Island experiences a marvelous adaptive radiation. After all, just about every niche is vacant, and there are a lot of niches. New Zealand did not produce a single species of Moa, but over a dozen, ranging in size from giants to tiny Kiwis and occupying a range of habitats. Madagascar flowered, producing several types of flightless birds, and an assortment of lemurs ranging from monkey like creatures to giants with the size and lifestyle of apes and sloths.

The Big Birds and Sesame Monsters that we see are both specialized creatures. It's likely that they had cousins, ground dwelling apelike creatures, and grasslands roaming giant birds, with midgets, behemoths, oddballs of every sort. It must have been a strange wonderland, with barely a predator, if any, to be found.

We can't identify the ultimate ancestors of the Big Birds, so this gives us no clue as to geography. But we can say with reasonable confidence that the Lorisidae which gave rise to the Sesame Monsters were indigenous to Africa and the southern reaches of Asia.

This suggests that our hypothetical island is most probably in the vicinity of the Indian Ocean. At the most westerly, it might be in the South China sea or around the East Indies. There's a lot of Islands in that area. We might also consider the Southern reaches of the Atlantic nearest Africa.

At the same time, we can easily rule out the North Pacific, the open South Pacific, the Southern reaches of the Indian Ocean, the North Atlantic, or anywhere near the Americas, Australia, Europe or Northern Asia.

If we assume, Snuffleupagus is from the same island, and is derived from the southern mammoth, primarily resident in Central Asia, we can mostly rule out African waters. Which puts us again in the Indian Ocean.

We can also speculate that it is far enough from the mainland that there aren't a lot of biological immigrants. The birds and loridae are not overwhelmed by new competitors, allowing them to evolve in strange directions. But on the other hand, it has to be close enough that dropping sea levels during the ice age, or perhaps geological processes, allow a temporary land bridge to form. So, perhaps a few dozen miles from the mainland, perhaps a couple of hundred. No more than that. That land bridge changes everything.

We can assume that if the mammoths crossed the land bridge, then it was principally a grasslands area. That stands to reason, the elevation is low and flat, drainage is probably rapid, the area's only above the water for a comparatively short time. The Mammoths are grassland creatures, so its likely that the flora and fauna of the land bridge was suitable to them. So, probably not mountain or rugged country, and probably not thick rain forest either.

But here's the problem. If mammoths can get across the land bridge, then other animals can too. Predators like wolves or lions, competitors like buffalo or antelope. The sheltered flora and fauna of Sesame Island are about to meet the ferocious competitors of the mainland.

The result is mass extinction. The outside mainland animals have been competing and evolving under harsher conditions in a much larger land area. Larger land masses mean greater populations, which in turn means greater mutation rates and more rapid change. It also means more competitors driving those changes.

Historically, the joining of two separated land masses has been disastrous for the animals of one of them. The best example is the joining of South America to North America, which itself was already connected to Eurasia. Before the merger, South America had produced a dizzying assortment of strange life forms, sloths the size of elephants, glyptodonts armoured like tanks, marsupial saber tooth tigers, giant predator birds, lions and wolves, imitations of elephants and horses, condors with twenty foot wingspans and giraffe-like creatures with elephant like trunks. When the two continents joined, 90% of South America's species were wiped out.

On a less dramatic scale, it has happened many times. The prior joining of North America to Asia resulted in extinction for a whole range of North American species. Human discoveries of Australia, Hawaii, New Zealand and Madagascar resulted in the extinctions of much of the slower megafauna of each of these places. Pity the poor dodo, he didn't survive meeting us.

So Sesame Island's remarkable diversity of species, the cousins to the Big Birds and the Sesame Monsters were probably all wiped out.

So why did the Sesame Monsters and the Big Birds survive? What was their secret?

I think that their survival gives us another clue confirming that the land bridge that connected Sesame Island to the mainland was mainly grassland. Why? Because the Sesame Monsters were rain forest tree dwellers, and the Big Birds were marshland creatures.

If the land bridge had included jungles and rain forests, then the invaders would have included tree climbing predators like leopards and jaguars as well as smaller cats and weasels. It would have included tree dwelling competitors like monkeys and apes, and the Sesame Monsters would have been driven to extinction.

The fact that they survived suggests that the land bridge was not carrying those species, and not supporting that habitat. By the same token, the slow moving Big Birds would have been vulnerable to marsh predators and competitors, had they been able to cross on the land bridge, but the habitats of the land bridge did not support those kinds of animals, so they never crossed.

So, as noted, what were probably crossing the land bridge were grasslands species, wiping out the Sesame Island life in their path, and precipitating a mass extinction of much of Sesame's animal life. But specialized as the interlopers were, they couldn't push into the secure habitats and niches of the Sesame species that were able to survive.

Now, here is where things get interesting. Neither the Sesame Monsters, nor the Snuffleupagus nor the Big Birds seem to have much natural fear. Rather, like the tortoises, birds and lizards of the Galapagos, and like the extinct moas and dodos, they seem to have no fear of man or predators. Their Island, like these others, was probably idyllically predator free.

In the case of the Big Birds and Sesame Monsters, that was probably their condition from the beginning. They grew up in Eden. But at the same time, there must have been predators that came over with the Snuffleupagus ancestors.

What happened to them? Population dynamics. Let's assume that the land bridge was temporary, open only for a relatively short time. Long enough for interlopers like mammoths to come over, but not for much longer than that.

The newly introduced predators encounter an island full of slow, fat, easy prey. So of course, they start killing and eating, and breeding. Their population skyrockets. Soon there are lots of predators.

Now, in normal ecologies, what you've got is a situation where predators and prey are relatively evenly matched. What this means is that the prey are able to reproduce fast enough, or to maintain large enough numbers, and the predators have enough trouble catching them, that the populations remain in rough balance.

On the other hand, when the predators have a huge advantage over the prey, then they kill and eat at will. The more they kill and eat, the more they can reproduce. Which means that the more of them there are to kill and eat and reproduce some more.

Until of course, the prey population starts to collapse. Then it starts to get interesting. The predator population keeps on growing, but the prey population is dropping. What this means is that hunting pressure by increasing numbers of predators on fewer and fewer individual prey keeps going up. No predator willingly starves to let his brother eat. Instead, the competition gets fierce and the pressure increases dramatically. The prey population implodes, with more and more predators chasing fewer and fewer prey, until the prey are literally extinct.

Bad news for predators on Sesame Island. So what do they do? Well, in the normal course of things, it would all straighten out in the long run. Sesame Island is being colonized by mainland herbivore species who have been the traditional prey. In fact, they've been kind of liking it, since most of the hunting pressure is on the easier to catch local species, they've been quietly moving into niches.

The trouble is that when the local species collapse, the predators are at the top of their boom cycle. There are lots and lots of predators, the ratio of predators of any sort to territory is a lot higher than normal. On the other hand, the population of interloping herbivores and prey species has not fully established itself. It takes a lot longer to grow a critter than it does to kill and eat. Over time, their population would expand and stabilize, but right now, they're underpopulated.

So, there's lots and lots of hungry, starving predators who have finished off the local species, and who are now going to work hard on the undersized population of new interloper species. Under major pressure, that interloper population too collapses.

And then the predators all starve, their population collapsing into local extinction.

Actually, this sort of thing happens more frequently than you'd like to think. A while back, someone charted populations of lynx's and rabbits in the wild and found their populations leapfrogged each other. Essentially, rabbits found the lynx's few and far between and the landscape green and chewy and started breeding like... well... rabbits. Lynx's would eat the rabbits. Their population would start to take off, the more rabbits to eat, the more lynx's.

Eventually though, the population of rabbits would reach the limits of food supply, but the population of lynx's would keep on swelling. Then suddenly, one day, there's way too many lynx's chasing too few rabbits, the rabbit population collapses, and a while later, the lynx population collapses. After a few years, the rabbits start the whole thing going again.

The difference, however, is that the lynx's and rabbits are inhabiting North America, so there's a lot more room to survive. The last lynx never manages to kill the last rabbit. The population collapse is never total. There's always a few on the margins somewhere who hang on to start the whole thing over again. But Sesame is an island, and not a very big one comparatively. It's ecology is in flux. This boom and bust is not part of a stable pattern. There on Sesame are a lot of metaphorical lynx's and not that many metaphorical rabbits, and when the last rabbit is killed, well, there ain't no more where that came from.

The fact is that extinction is not an uncommon phenomenon, and it doesn't usually take an asteroid hitting, or a super-killer species (like us), or even two continents joining. Most times, extinction comes as a result of painting yourself into a corner, and island life makes that a much bigger risk.

But anyway, back to Sesame Island's new population of immigrant predators: There's nothing left on the island to eat. The only prey are inaccessible, the Sesame Monsters sitting high atop rain forest canopies, the Big Birds standing in the swamps with their eggs tucked under their arms or the

.ammoths who are just too damned big and ornery to take down.

So the predators starve. Or they eat each other, which cuts down the population but only postpones starvation. And eventually, no more predators.

Of course, while that happens, Sesame Island probably goes through a mass extinction, as all the vulnerable species are killed off. The ones that survived are in the niches that the predators could not get too easily, such as tree tops and swamps. Or were big enough, like the mammoths, that they were immune.

Sesame Island goes back to its sleepy ways, but now there are very few species. The species that are left, are quite advanced and sophisticated, well adapted for their niches.

Trapped on the Island, unhindered by possible predators, and with all the smaller mammal rivals hunted to extinction, the southern mammoths start reducing, ending up as the pygmy Snuffleupagus, who proves to be a quiet and genial neighbor, uninterested in competing with or bothering the Big Birds or the Sesame Monsters.

But there are all sorts of newly vacated niches. There's neither predators nor competition to keep the Sesame Monsters from moving into these niches. And in occupying these niches, there is an adaptive pressure to change, to make the fit a little better.

So once again, they speciate. But the new species or new occupiers on the niches will be variations on the survivors. So, for instance, we might see ground dwelling bush Sesame Monsters developing robust teeth for chomping on tougher vegetation, or different patterns of fur, or even furless Sesame

Monsters. New features might include horns, larger or smaller eyes, or other specialized adaptions.

Now, we have to make some important observations on this speciation. The variant Sesame Monsters have hundreds of thousands of years, or even millions of years, to adapt to their new niches, so we can expect to see some changes. Nevertheless, even a few million years of adaptation will not give us the diversity of forms and species we would see in a non-impacted landscape.

I mean, look at a modern landscape, and what do you see? Rabbits, antelopes, rats, deer, foxes, cats, mice, wolves and so on. There are a series of creatures occupying different niches with radically different forms, behaviours, strategies and lifestyles. Part of this is driven by the fact that they're occupying different ecological niches. But a large part of it is also that they have long and differing lineages. There's twenty million years between dogs and cats, forty million years between a rabbit and an antelope, there's eighty million years between a rat and a deer. All the animals in the landscape are coming from different ancestor species, who in turn came from different ancestors and so on, and they've had tens upon tens of millions of years to develop apart.

Now, in contrast, take a look at dogs. Specifically, take a look at all the bewildering forms of dogs, from St. Bernards and Great Danes, Sheepdogs and Collies, to Huskies, Retrievers, Poodles and Chihuahua, we see a diversity that almost mimics a natural landscape in some ways.

The key is 'almost' and 'in some ways.' Each breed of dog no matter how colossal, or deviant, no matter whether the ponderous newfoundlander, the streamlined greyhound or elongated dachshund remains clearly a dog. The skeletal and skull and foot morphology is the same, the dental structure and dietary parameters are the same, the brain structure, the ingrained behaviour and social processes are consistent. No matter how far a particular breed of dog pushes the range, the creature is still a dog, and clearly one with its peers.

The finches of the Galapagos underwent an adaptive radiation that was remarkable in its own right. But the finches clearly remained finches.

So, the point is that the Sesame Monsters, even when adapting to new niches, will still remain Sesame Monsters. They might get bigger or smaller, sport horns, develop larger teeth. But in most physical ways, including in most cases, size, general proportions, skeletal features, internal anatomy, neural wiring and behavioural traits.... the apple is not going to fall far from the tree.

For instance, most will probably fall into the same size ranges as normal Sesame Monsters, most will be left handed, most will be four fingered. Where an animal departs from the norm in some specific way, it may conform to the norms in most other respects. The differences and departures will be cosmetic. After all, the divergence is from a highly adapted, relatively specialized and sophisticated animal, and although they're moving into new niches, there's no geographical isolation, so its unlikely that we're going to get true speciation. All the variants will be closely related, and perhaps capable of interbreeding. So at best, we may be looking at subspecies, or perhaps merely variant breeds within a species.

This allows us to speculate a bit. For instance, the drummer, Animal, may be a bush browser, developing heavy teeth for chomping. Is Rolf really a dog or simply a ground dwelling, long eared Sesame Monster who is occupying a gorilla's niche and bulking up? Is Kermit really a frog, or simply a marsh adapted Sesame Monster whose particular adaptations are furlessness, greenish skin and a wedge shaped mouth?

We can expect that the same processes would take place for the descendants of Big Bird, the main line of Big Birds will continue to dominate. But the opening of new niches will allow for adaptation and speciation. We might see new or specialized offshoots of the Big Birds, including small dark forms with crooked beaks occupying some peculiar niche and with an affinity for chickens, or perhaps a mid-sized, solitary, hook-nosed, bald bird.

In short, what we would be seeing, potentially, is a proliferation of the non-standard Sesame Monsters, the variant creature types. In some cases, analysis of their physical differences might allow us to guess at their niches and lifestyles. In other cases, it's a wild stab in the dark. But the point is that we can place them biologically within the evolutionary history of Sesame Island.

Intelligence and Language among the Monsters

The creatures of Sesame Street are apparently unique in nature for their linguistic abilities. Unlike just about every other animal, they both speak and understand human language, conversing on levels approaching our own.

I say apparently unique because on closer examination, there is both more and less than meets the eye. The Sesame creatures are not operating on adult human levels. Big Bird, for instance, has been described as cognitively equivalent to a six year old. Grover is arguably less sophisticated. Others might be more. But on the whole, the Sesame Monsters and their associates display reasoning capacities roughly on a par with children.

Well, not to put too fine a face on it, but some particularly smart dogs have been classified as roughly equivalent to twelve year olds. Apes, elephants, dolphins, certain breeds of monkeys, parrots and perhaps even lines of felines have all demonstrated capacities for cognitive abilities, problem solving, memory, sequencing and other reasoning skills that achieve the same or better ranges than the Sesame Street monsters and their ilk.

Even the linguistic ability is not singular. The average dog, has a capacity to learn or be trained to a couple of hundred commands or words. There was one dog with an understanding vocabulary of four hundred words, and who understood grammar to the extent that words in different orders would mean different things to it.

Studies with American sign language, or computer symbology indicate that chimpanzees and gorillas could master and use vocabularies of several hundred words.

A parrot has been shown to use language conceptually, not simply repeating words, but understanding that words have meanings and using words to express its desires and feelings.

Even the lowly vervet monkey has been shown to have a vocabulary of words which express or describe different animals, allowing them to distinguish threats.

So in that sense, there's nothing spectacularly unusual about the Sesame Monsters and their associates. The range of intelligence and linguistic comprehension that they display, while remarkable and definitely at the high end, is found repeatedly within the animal world.

But there's one way in which the Sesame Monsters differ from their other peers in the natural world: You can't shut them up. The Sesame Monsters are actively linguistic, and this is an important distinction.

Chimps, for instance, can be taught American sign language, and can communicate in this way. But the remarkable thing about films and videos of signing chimps is how taciturn they are. Although they can communicate, they generally don't feel motivated to do it. In videos, we see trainers and teachers constantly coaxing and cajoling them, trying to get them to sign or communicate. On their own, they do relatively little signing, though they will use it to express wants and desires.

Although Chimps have linguistic capacity, they aren't actively linguistic. They show no particular linguistic affinity or impulse in the wild. Neither do gorillas. Wolves arguably have a similar linguistic capacity to dogs, they have a range of vocalizations and highly organized social and hunting behaviour, but they do not make the jump to language. Parrots can learn to understand and use speech, but there's no indication that wild parrots have any use for it.

There seems to be something missing in most animals that have high linguistic capacity. Something that even a babbling child possesses. A child has a language impulse, humans have language impulses. We talk even when there's nothing to talk about and no one to talk to. Beyond capacity, there must be a drive to use that capacity, and that's what's missing.

Apart from man, alone of all the varieties of animals, the creatures of Sesame Island have not only the capacity, but the impulse to use it.

Why is that?

Primate Intelligence on Sesame Island

Dawn of Cthulhu – Page 169

Before we go into language, let's take a moment to examine the utility and nature of intelligence. After all, the Sesame Monsters closest evolutionary analogues are sloths and koalas. Each is a remarkable creature in its own right, but neither are rocket scientists. Why are the Sesame Monsters smart, and sloths stupid? What's going on?

Partly, it may be that the Sesame Monsters come from good breeding. They're an offshoot of primates, an evolutionary line that was selecting for intelligence all the way along. But even that is at best only a partial answer. The Sesame Monsters are a shoot off the slow branch of that family tree after all. But why are primates smart anyway?

What it comes down to is lifestyle. Most primates, most monkeys and apes, are frugivores. That is, their main diet is fruit.

This has its ups and downs. On the one hand, fruit is a very high value, high energy diet. You get a lot of bang for the buck. Your average grass eating herbivore has to consume constantly, it has to eat huge quantities of grass and leaves, which are low value, low energy diets. They also need special adaptations, gut bacteria, multiple stomachs, all sorts of remarkable things to be able to process tough vegetation.

On the other hand, grass and leaves can be found just about anywhere. It's a reliable, universal foodstuff that you can find plenty of and that allows you to grow some very big animals.

Fruit? That's a different story.

It's possible for a frugivore to starve to death in a forest, if there are no fruit trees. Or it can starve to death if there are no fruit trees in season while its hungry. Indeed, for a fruit eater, most of a lush forest will be as sterile and inedible as a desert. Its diet is highly specialized, and so 99% of the vegetation in that environment is useless to it.

This is where intelligence in monkeys and apes come in. To be a successful frugivore, you need to know where the fruit trees are. You can't just go around trying trees randomly, you might starve to death before you find the right one. You need to be able to find them, you need to be able to remember them, and you need to be able to place them in reference to your environment so you can find them again. That takes some pretty substantial mental mapping and requires a bit of brain power.

More than that, fruit trees tend to have a specific season. Come to a tree too early and there's nothing but twigs and maybe blossoms. Come a little later, and the fruit's started, but its not ripe. Come too late, and its past its season, the fruit is gone or rotten. So not only does our smart little monkey have to remember where that tree is and how to find it, but he's got to be able to figure out what it's got and when its in season. That requires a bit more mental mapping, including adding a time dimension, or going by environmental cues, either of which requires more brain power.

Of course, different kinds of fruit have different seasons. Our smart little monkey has to eat year round. So not only must he be able to find a tree, and find it in season, but he's got to do it with a lot of different kinds of fruit trees, and different ages of trees in different locations, in order to build up a year round diet.

All of which calls for sophisticated mental processes: Memory, positional mapping, inferences from environmental cues, time sorting, categorization, making distinctions. Complicated stuff. The result is that monkeys have to be pretty smart. And apes like orang-utans, chimps and gibbons, who are bigger and hungrier frugivores are smarter still.

When we look at parrots, we find that parrots are ecologically occupying the same niches as monkeys. They're arboreal frugivores, and they have to do the same tricks that monkeys do in order to find their meal. The result is that parrots are among, if not the absolutely, the smartest birds around.

So, turning to our Sesame Monsters, is this what is going on? I think so. We've already determined from their mouth and jaw structure, their body shape, that they are very specialized feeders. A little bit more diverse than the average frugivore, in that their diet probably contains more tender leaves and shoots. But it is still highly specialized. So they need to develop the same basic set of intellectual tools that monkeys and apes use.

Indeed, they're slow moving in comparison to monkeys and apes. This means that moving from one place to another in search of food takes longer and consumes more energy, so their risk factor is higher. A monkey can scamper its heart out and search through dozens of trees in the time it would take a Sesame Monster to explore two or three. This is important, a Sesame Monster just doesn't have the time or spare energy to be stupid. Being a slow-mover means he's got to be even smarter about how and where to find food.

But the basic intelligence processing is the same. Indeed, if we look at transcripts of Sesame Monsters speech, it is remarkable how transparent it is. Sesame Monsters are almost obsessively focused on the sorts of tasks or skill sets that a frugivore needs to find food. They are fascinated with the difference between one thing and another, with distinguishing objects from groups, they're obsessed with timing, with location, with finding and with counting.

In the subjects that they talk about, the subjects that fascinate and excite them, we find the blueprint for the skills and the intellectual abilities that sustain their lifestyle in the wild. It's as if it is hard wired into their neural structure.

This raises interesting questions. Are the Sesame Monsters truly intelligent creatures, or are they biological robots, acting out evolutionary programming hard-wired into their neural net? They display various intellectual skills, but these skills, and the impulse to use them, the drive to use them, seems to be based in evolution. They love to count, they love to sort, they are excited to distinguish objects not by choice, but because this is what their wiring compels. Are they creatures of reason, or merely instinct?

For that matter, are we? As humans, we love to celebrate our intelligence and free will. But looking at the Sesame Monsters, whose unquestioned intelligence seems selected by and driven by instinct, we have to wonder. We can look at these creatures mental tools and see how clearly these tools are at the service of their biology. But what about us? Are we fooling ourselves? Are we, like the Sesame Monsters, merely creatures of instinct, our intelligence merely a tool for hardwired biological drives?

There is no easy answer, only the dim mirror that the Sesame Monsters hold up for us. In them, we see a diminished, smaller, simpler version of ourselves. Perhaps we should not be so proud. We may be closer to them than we would like.

Intelligence - the Big Birds and Snuffleupagus

Big Bird is not a frugivore, or perhaps not solely one. Yet Big Bird's intelligence seems roughly on a par with that of the Sesame Monsters.

Why is he so smart?

I think that the answer must be because in many ways, Big Bird's evolution is a parallel development. Like the primate frugivores, Big Bird's diet is obviously highly specialized. Big Bird probably consumes a number of items in his environment, but he's not a generalized feeder. Rather, he feeds widely through narrow ranges. Frogs, fish, certain kinds of invertebrates, certain kinds of plants, shoots, fruit, etc. These foods are to be found scattered through a complex environment. Some may be intensely seasonal, some may require sophisticated food gathering techniques and even cooperative behaviour.

The long and the short of it is that the Big Birds, like the monkeys, must make mental maps of their environment. They must be able to infer from cues and clues. They must understand and use seasonality and timing. And they must do this in an environment which is, in many ways, more complex and diverse than the jungle canopies.

We've noted that parrots are the bird equivalent of monkeys. The Big Birds are the bird equivalent of apes or hominids.

There are differences of course. For primates, its all about finding the right tree, and then you eat like a king. Primate food gathering is all about the big score. For the Big Birds, each day is an exercise in problem solving, every day finding a new basket of small food items to make up your meal. For the most part, the Big Birds do not make big scores. They make lots of little scores. They likely increase their chances by acting in groups, sharing information and feeding strategies, even sharing finds.

Perhaps for this reason, transcripts of Big Bird conversations do not show the obsessive joy in things like counting, distinguishing or sorting. Sesame Monster conversations are usually 'object directed,' they want to talk about things: objects, cookies, toys, and the nature and characteristics of these things, what kind are they, how are they different from each other, how many of them are there. These things excite them, it fascinates them, they light right up.

In contrast, the conversation of Big Bird is not nearly so excitable. Big Bird does talk about objects, he does count them, he makes distinctions between categories, and shows all the same mental tools. But he doesn't bring the same enthusiasm to them. He doesn't get excited the way that Sesame Monsters get. Take musical instruments, a Sesame Monster would be fascinated by the numbers and types of instruments. Big Bird would be interested in the music.

Instead, Big Bird's conversation is more relationship driven. He wants to talk to people around him, rather than about things. He is excited by the prospect of making friends or seeing friends, he focuses on being with others, doing things with them. Big Bird survives in his environment by focusing on relationships with others in that environment, and exchanging resources and information.

Thus, while evolution produces a comparable intelligence in Big Bird, the orientation and directions of that intelligence seems quite distinct.

The big puzzle on Sesame Island, of course, is the Snuffleupagus. Why is this animal intelligent?

Unlike the Big Birds and the Sesame Monsters, the Snuffleupagus is a browser or grazer. The demands of finding food are simply not as complex and do not require the same sorts of highly refined mental tools.

In one way, the answer is easier. We have to justify Sesame Monster and Big Bird intelligence literally from the ground up, as these animals represent their own evolutionary lines. On the other hand, the Snuffleupagus is a relatively recent descendant of mammoths and elephants.

Obviously, he gets his intelligence from his ancestors, the mammoths. But that begs the question of why mammoths and elephants are as smart as they are. Certainly not from fear of predators, and certainly not from the need to find food. Why are they smart?

Maybe simply because they're big? Big critters, big brains? Possibly it's a fluke, the hyper development of their trunk with the immense complexity of nerves and muscles triggered highly sophisticated brains to handle it, much like acoustic sonar seems to have triggered brain complexity in dolphins and whales.

One possible explanation for elephant intelligence is social complexity. These creatures are so huge that they're hard on their immediate environment. A population can strip an area bare easily. They're so massive that it is difficult to move easily from one area to another. At the same time, at their size level, conflict is extremely dangerous. It's all too easy, if you're an Elephant, for things to get out of hand. Remember, it's all fun and games when someone loses an eye. Elephants can't afford to let things get that far.

So possibly intelligence offers options to organize themselves socially in order to minimize conflict, manage the group and the group relationships, and cope with other groups. Basically, to make sure that everything and everyone is peaceful, because the absence of peace is bad for everyone.

Interestingly, transcripts of Snuffleupagus conversation betrays almost no interest in the subjects that interest and excite Sesame Monsters.

Instead, Snuffleupagus speech is almost wholly social. But it differs from Big Bird speech in that Big Bird's social speech is extroverted. Big Bird is always interested in making a new friend, and meeting the friends of friends.

Snuffy's speech pattern and interests show almost no extroversion. He is friendly, but not very curious. It seems that Big Bird's friendship is important to him, but he has little interest in extending his social network or meeting Big Bird's friends. For a protracted period, Snuffleupagus had so little interest (though no particular sign of fear) that he would simply wander off when the direct social bonding ended.

For Snuffleupagus, social interaction is not a tool for feeding, for learning about the things you need, the places you need, the tricks and treats, rather, it's about ensuring the stability of the environment. As long as that environment is stable and comforting, Snuffleupagus doesn't need more.

Towards a Theory of Monster Language

Okay, so we know why they're smart. But why do they talk? And why do they seem so bent upon talking?

Sesame Monsters intelligence derives from the same evolutionary drivers as monkeys and apes. But monkeys and apes, while they have linguistic capacity, lack linguistic impulse. So what's the deal here.

A large part of it seems to be the subtle differences between Sesame Monsters and monkeys and apes. As we've noted, Sesame Monsters are slow moving primates. This poses all sorts of problems for them.

For one thing, conflict and aggression are tricky. Most animals, including monkeys and apes, employ aggression with each other, and have a series of graduated stages by which aggression is expressed, from threat display to outright conflict.

The environment and biology of Sesame Monsters pose unique difficulties. For one thing, they're slow moving creatures in arboreal environments. So they can simply move away from conflict. It's hard to sustain a fight if one side or the other simply walks away. The aggressor cannot force or attack, all they can do is pursue at a walk. So the attempt at aggression results in a protracted low speed chase, clambering slowly from one branch to the next, around and around and around. That's not particularly useful or efficient. You can't drive a rival off a tree or away from a mate or establish dominance. All you can do is go round in circles until you get tired.

The other thing is that these are relatively heavy, arboreal creatures. Falls can be easily fatal, or result in serious injury. So the sort of close proximity where real aggression can take place, is far more serious and dangerous than for other animals on the ground, or for lighter agile animals in the trees.

The result is that aggression has almost no utility among Sesame Monsters. It's largely futile and ineffective, and on rare occasions when it can be effective, it's so dangerous as to not be worth the risk. The result is that aggression forms literally no part of the Sesame Monsters behavioural repertoire. We see this even today on Sesame Street itself, where the monsters, while curious and outgoing, display almost no aggression towards humans or each other.

Okay, so they're pacifists. So what? Patience. We're getting there.

Without aggression to manage their social relationships, the Sesame Monsters still have to compete for food, resources and mates. They still have to deal with each other. They still have to expend time and energy moving from one food source to another, food sources which may already be harvested or partially harvested.

As we've noted, remember that these are slow moving creatures. So the relative energy and time investment in moving from one food source to another is much greater than for monkeys and apes. They have less room to make mistakes and fewer options to explore. The Sesame Monsters need information about their environment, and complex information, in order to make decisions as to where to go, what to do, and how long to stay.

This is where language comes in. Language is explicitly a conflict avoidance and resource exploitation strategy. A Sesame Monster in a tree can determine, fairly accurately, without resort to language, where the nearest fruit trees are, how to reach them, and when they'll be in season. But he cannot determine, without language, without actually going there, how bountiful the tree is, whether the season is early or late or on time, whether it is harvested out or diseased, whether it already has Sesame Monsters feeding, how many there are, how much can the tree sustain, how rich or untapped it is, and how easy or difficult the feeding is.

The only way a Sesame Monster can know this easily is if another Sesame Monster tells him. With that information, a

Sesame Monster can decide, very quickly, whether to proceed to that tree, whether it is still rich enough to support him, whether he should stay, or try another tree, and which trees might have already been harvested. It allows complex decisions to be made as to where to go and how to proceed.

It's in the interest of other Sesame Monsters to share this information. If a tree has excess capacity, then a Sesame Monster cannot horde it. The fruit will spoil eventually. So he has no interest in keeping rivals or competitors away. Indeed, other animals represent potential mates and potential sources of information. So it is worthwhile to share, if he can.

If, on the other hand, the tree is already overpopulated, or already harvested out, then a new animal joining the feeding will be a problem. Under other circumstances, aggression might drive the interloper away, or result in the original tree feeder being driven off. However aggression isn't an effective option for Sesame Monsters, they're too heavy to risk falling and too slow to risk chasing each other around.

Much better to be able to inform the interloper as to the prospects. An interloper can then determine that there's sufficient excess capacity to make joining the tree worthwhile. Or they can determine that despite being in season and being fecund, there's insufficient capacity. No need for aggression, just a friendly conversation about whether it is worth while.

Sharing or giving information reduces or eliminates potential conflict and minimizes competition while maximizing social and mating opportunities.

Linguistic impulse allows the individual Sesame Monsters to maximize their feeding strategies, quickly allowing them to determine local resources and population, and allowing more information to pursue long term feeding strategies... ie, about the next tree, the one after that, and the one after that.

Biologically, they have an incentive, not only to obtain information, but to share it. They have a biological imperative to talk to each other.

Co-Evolving Language

For one animal to evolve a linguistic impulse on Sesame Island is amazing. For three of them is little short of miraculous. What is going on here?

We know that both elephants and parrots have linguistic capacity, if not linguistic impulse. We can assume that the Snuffleupagus inherits the linguistic capacity the same way he inherits intelligence from his elephantine forbears.

The Big Birds have no place to inherit from. But comparing other species, we can infer that the complex and richly textured environment, the wide range of narrow foodstuffs, the need for nest building and egg protection, the need for co-operative and complex feeding strategies, and the need to teach those strategies, and the small but complex social groups encourages both complex intelligence and linguistic capacity.

But why did these animals make the jump to speech? From linguistic capacity to linguistic impulse? Why did it allow them to make the jump from having the capacity to actually wanting or needing to exercise that capacity? And why three unrelated species in the same or overlapping time frames and to roughly the same level of ability?

What we have here is a case of co-evolution. Co-evolution is common in nature. In its simplest form, cheetahs encourage the evolution of faster antelopes because the slower ones get eaten, and antelopes encourage the evolution of faster cheetahs because the slower ones starve.

But there are very complex forms of co-evolution as well. Sharks and remoras, multi-species herds, symbiotic relationships. The most remarkable example of co-evolution are bees and flowering plants. Essentially, flowering plants and pollinating insects have evolved together, each adapting to the other in furtherance of their goals. Co-evolution has reached points where there are certain flowering plants that may be pollinated only by a specific species of insect.

Co-evolution takes place in an environment where two species overlap, and where the adaptive pressures on one species helps to shape the other species response. A species finds that the adaptations of another species give it opportunities, and adapts further to exploit those opportunities.

So, how does language co-evolve on Sesame Island?

It goes back to the mass extinction on Sesame Island in which the proto-Snuffleupagus came to the Island and in which many of the local indigenous species were wiped out, along with the interlopers who would have normally moved into those niches. The influx of predators, as we've noted, helped to wipe out the local species, and then a hyper-population of predators wiped out an incoming and inadequate population of interlopers, before itself crashing to extinction.

What this means is that Sesame Island was inhabited by a handful of survivor species in secure untouched niches, and that there were a whole lot of new niches which were open and vacant.

Open niches invite occupation. The Big Birds began to explore beyond their marshes, to rivers, grasslands and borderline rain forests. The Sesame Monsters began to explore beyond their core habitats. Even the Snuffleupagus broadened their niches. This meant that the Big Birds and the Sesame Monsters were frequently coming into contact, and indeed, were often overlapping in niches or habitats that were relatively poor for them and required active intelligence by each to exploit effectively.

The Big Birds, moving into a series of strange environments which they needed to actively observe and understand the resources available, discovered in Sesame Monsters a series of little walking databases of useful information. Obviously they were intelligent enough to teach each other feeding and behaviour strategies, which means that they were intelligent enough to learn by observation. So they were capable of learning from observing Sesame Monsters, and eventually, found substantial advantages in being able to decode the Sesame Monsters communication.

It was probably a long adaptive process, first appreciating different kinds of signals, and then increasingly refining meaning from these signals. But in the end, the information as to foods, locations, distances and other issues could be quite useful.

The ability to communicate with or talk to Sesame Monsters increased the ability to gain useful information from them. For their part, the Sesame Monsters also found a competitive advantage in being able to talk to and obtain information from the Big Birds. It exposed them to a wider variety of food sources and food source techniques in more habitats.

The Snuffleupagus in their widening niches, and in contact with both Big Birds and Sesame Monsters were also brought along linguistically. They too found an adaptive advantage to being able to decode the conversations going on around them.

Of course, the Snuffleupagus were more conservative in their exploration of niches. Perhaps for this reason, they seem to have co-evolved the least linguistic impulse. For Snuffleupagus information from Sesame Monsters as to the quality and distribution of fruit trees, while useful for occasional feeding under trees, was not vital. Information exchange as to habitats or resources simply did not confer the same scale of benefit. Social information exchange with the Big Birds was more valuable, but the two species, while their habitats might overlap, were not competing for or sharing many food resources. Bottom line, while there was advantage, there was less advantage for them.

Perhaps for this reason, the Snuffleupagus linguistic impulse seems less pronounced than in the two other species. Examining transcripts of Snuffleupagus speech and comparing them to Big Bird or Sesame Monster speech, we find that the Snuffleupagus employ fewer words, they speak with simpler syntax, they are less voluntary or impulsive with speech, they speak less often. Snuffleupagus display little of the enthusiasm for speech shown by Big Birds or Sesame Monsters, and almost none of the obsessional excitement of Sesame Monsters. Nevertheless, the fact that they have linguistic impulse to any degree remains remarkable.

The question arises as to why, if the three Sesame Island species could evolve and co-evolve speech, then why hasn't a similar phenomena occurred in respect of man? We are after all sophisticated language users and we have relationships with many species with at least some linguistic capacity.

Why don't elephants talk to Mahouts? Why don't dogs converse with their masters? Why haven't the wild orang-utan or chimps which coexist with aboriginal humans not picked up even rudimentary communication? It would be a great advantage for orangs or chimps to be able to communicate with humans, if for no other reason than to reduce hunting and increase scavenging opportunities.

There seem to be two answers to this question. One is that the linguistic impulse and linguistic capacity of humans so far outstrips the animals around us that there's just no catching up. Our linguistic use is so complex and wide ranging, and other animals abilities are so limited in comparison, that there is no real advantage.

Our signal to noise ratio is simply far too lopsided, too much of what we say is too complex and too irrelevant, the potential useful information is too hard to fish out. Linguistically, we're flying around on fighter jets, and they're trying to get skateboards working.

In contrast, it appears that the Sesame Monsters, Big Birds and Snuffleupagus were all fairly close to the same level. The Sesame Monsters were never so advanced that the Big Birds and Snuffleupagus were unable to catch up, and once these other animals became linguistic, they all continued to develop together. The linguistic gulf was not so huge as to be unbridgeable, and there were immediate advantages to even minimal bridging.

The other answer is simply that there hasn't been time. We can identify the period of linguistic co-evolution as sometime after the land bridge to Sesame Island, the colonization by Southern Mammoths, the introduction of predators and mass extinction, the closure of the land bridge and the subsequent expansion of the prosimians into vacant niches.

Dawn of Cthulhu – Page 185

We don't know when exactly this happened. But we do know that the Southern Mammoth, the progenitor species for the Snuffleupagus, existed between four and one million years ago. So we know that the different Sesame Island species had at least several hundred thousand years, and perhaps as long as a few million years, to co-evolve language. They have been talking to each other for a long time.

Compare this to humanity. Our species, Homo Sapiens is only a hundred thousand years old. Related species might push us back a million tops, but we have no idea how far back our language use goes.

Of species hanging around with us, the earliest were dogs, who have only been associated with humans for somewhere between 40,000 and 15,000 years. Most other species (most of them without linguistic capacity) have only been domesticated within the last twelve thousand years. Most of them much more recently. Elephant semi-domestication is almost certainly less than 5000 years old. So in this sense, there's been almost no time to co-evolve language.

Despite this, there does seem to be some indication of language co-evolution in early stages. Recent studies have shown that dogs seem to have slightly more linguistic capacity than wolves. While it is difficult to make statistical comparisons, dogs seem to show a larger innate capacity for vocabulary or commands than wolves, and more aptitude for understanding sequence in that vocabulary (sequence of course, being the key component of grammar - the notion that the order of words affects their meaning - itself a key component of language).

One interesting datum suggests that there might be something significant going on: If you point at something, a dog will look at what you are pointing at. A wolf won't, the gesture is meaningless to it. Dogs have learned to read us in ways that wolves cannot.

So who knows, perhaps in another fifty or a hundred thousand years of association, dogs may themselves become a linguistic species. And perhaps within that time frame, or sometime after that, elephants, if they survive, may join the club.

In the meantime, we share our world with three species remarkably gifted with the ability to talk to us. That they are not on our level does not reduce the importance and significance of these gifts. In these creatures we see our reflection, the differences between us fade away before the common heritage that we share in inhabiting this small world together. The gulf between them and us is merely one of degree rather than nature, and the gulf between them and the rest of the natural world is again, a simple matter of degrees. Through them we understand that we are a part of this world, their world, our world, and not above it. Our superiority does not separate us, but rather, allows us to appreciate and understand our responsibility for these, our kindred children of Earth.

The Monsters in New York

Now one last thought, before we depart. How do we get from Sesame Island somewhere off the Asian shores of the Indian Ocean to Sesame Street in New York?

Well, it's probably a mistake to assume that Sesame Island goes undiscovered. Instead, if we looked around to folklore or fiction, I suspect that we'd find reports or stories of a mysterious Island of talking animals.

The region around the Indian ocean's Asian shorelines, the most likely location for Sesame Island, was relatively well traveled for at least the last fifteen hundred years. Malays and Indonesians settled the Indonesian archipelago. Malayan seafarers colonized Madagascar approximately 1500 to 2000 years ago.

Sometime after that, Muslim sailed along the shorelines of India to make converts as far east as the Philippine Moro Islands. In turn, Indian merchants and traders dotted the east coast of Africa, establishing cities like Zanzibar. The Chinese, during the middle ages, established a huge fleet which sailed along the coasts reaching as far as Africa.

So its likely that Sesame Island could be locally known. On the other hand, the sailors of India, China, Africa and Malaya tended not to go far from land. They traveled great distances, but most of their sailing expeditions were short jaunts along well established routes, hugging the shorelines. Thus, large islands in the deep Indian Ocean, such as Mauritius, Reunion, the Crozet and Kerguelen archipelagos and others remained undiscovered until European sailors arrived.

Sesame Island was perhaps a few dozen to a couple of hundred miles from the mainland. It's likely that it would have been known of, or discovered or rediscovered from time to time. On the other hand, depending on wind and current, it might well have escaped discovery for much of its history.

Even if it was discovered, we could conceive that it was far enough away that it was not reachable by aboriginal tribes, but only by the more civilized sailing societies. These societies would have encountered a strange land of talking, humanlike animals. They may well have chosen to give it a wide berth. Many of the strange fauna of Madagascar were left strictly alone by the Malay settlers, described as tabu or supernatural.

It's worth noting as well that even in the event of human settlement, much of the island habitats would not be troubled by human agriculture and subsistence forestry. Indeed, humans were particular in the territories that they settled. Agricultural or fishing villages generally didn't tend to locate in deep marshes, or tropical rainforests. There might have been some habitat infringement, and perhaps new species and diseases introduced. But the Sesame Island creatures would have had centuries, perhaps even millennia to adapt, and the most vulnerable life forms were already long extinct.

From there, we can assume that Sesame Island was discovered by Portugese traders in the 16th century, by the Dutch in the 17th century. They were probably described by sailors early on. Specimens, living or dead, would be transported back to Europe in the 16th or 17th century, but they would have been mere curiosities.

Eventually the Island would taken as a colonial territory by either the French, British or Dutch in the 18th or 19th century. The colonial nations of the period from the 16th through the 19th centuries were more interested in profit and commerce than science or novelty. The members of the various Island races might have started showing up in European royal courts, zoos and circuses as early as the 18th and 19th centuries.

It would not have been until the late era of the 19th century, say from circa 1860 onwards, and the growth of educated and literate European and American middle classes that the Sesame creatures, probably named Muy-Pahts from the Thai language, or Mu-Pets based on post-Darwinian notions of lost continents such as Lemuria and Mu, would have become popular.

From that point, there would have been a serious public demand for the creatures in zoos or circuses, or for private collectors. Darwin had become popular, and the creatures would have been in great demand as object lessons and missing links.

During this period, particularly 1870 to 1950, anthropomorphized animals were popular, thus monkeys were made to wear little suits, trained bears wore hats, apes were put in dresses. The popular motif was to have animals dressing and acting in parodies of human behaviour. In this light, the Mu-Pets, particularly the Sesame Monsters were popular in the roles. This was a period where many Mu-Pets were absorbed into human culture, dressed in human clothes, taught human roles and trained to enact scenes of human pageantry, from the Wild West to the age of Buccaneers.

There's a question of course, as to how well they would do in captivity. They were fundamentally wild animals occupying specialized habitat with particular diets. Moving them into the stressful situations of circuses and zoos would have put pressure on them, exposed them to parasites, diseases, malnutrition and obesity from bad diets and chronic social stress. So many of the captured animals, particularly of the first generation, would not have done well.

The evidence from Sesame Street the television show is that these are long lived creatures. Possibly their lives are equivalent to human spans, or even greater. They would tend to reproduce slowly, and their young would probably be vulnerable. So its likely that hunting pressure to fill the burgeoning needs of zoos and circuses would probably have impacted the Island population.

So how does this explain the Sesame Street colony of Mu-Pets? The most likely explanation is that they were from a circus that went bankrupt or otherwise failed somewhere in the 1920's or 1930's.

Most of the circus performers would have gone on to other circuses or found normal jobs. The dangerous or unwieldy animals would have either been purchased by other circuses, found their way to zoos or been put down. Indeed, if times were hard on circuses, it would have probably been cheapest to simply kill off the wild animals.

The exceptions would have been horses, who could have been re-deployed for other work, and the Sesame Monsters, who by and large, were non-aggressive, posed no threats to the community at large, and were small enough (even the Big Birds) that they could thrive scavenging in urban environments. Also, its damned hard to shoot something that can talk to you, and whose manner is so childlike.

Another possibility is that these animals were pets who either escaped or were abandoned.

Indeed, there's now a well established history of exotic pets who become all the rage, such as baby alligators, Vietnamese pot bellied pigs, parrots. However, over time, the novelty wears off, peoples circumstances or interests changes, the pets grow too big or aggressive, or for one reason or another, the pets are disposed of, one way or another.

Baby alligators were flushed down the toilet. Vietnamese Pot-Bellied pigs were put down. Parrots are an interesting case because they often outlive the lifestyles or commitments of their owners.

One of my old neighbors had a parrot colony in their living room. They had more than a dozen birds of almost as many species, ranging from cockatoos to macaws to norwegian blues. They didn't set out to collect parrots, but what happened was that from time to time, people who had parrots found that they didn't want to keep them. Either they were changing jobs or homes, going through divorces, having medical or financial problems, or simply bored with the birds. The thing is, these critters don't die. Their life spans are comparable to humans, which means that parrots will probably outlive most marriages, will outlive careers, will outlive bachelorhood, and most of your child's adolescence. Owning a parrot is a lifetime commitment, in an age where a lot of people have trouble signing a lease for a year. Anyway, the bottom line is that people wanted to get rid of their parrots, and so they'd just sort of dump them on my neighbor, which is how he got such an extraordinary collection of birds.

So here's an alternate explanation for the Sesame Street colony. Perhaps they're simply abandoned pets who wound up congregating for their need for society and companionship. Indeed, people bent on abandoning their Sesame Monsters might well drop them off at a colony or near other wild monsters so that they can learn to fend for themselves.

Or they might have been dropped off at some informal sanctuary, like my parrot-keeping neighbors, and then simply made a gradual transition to independence, or perhaps outlived their sanctuary-keeper.

Or possibly, they're simply escapees who sought each other out and founded or joined wild colonies.

One thing is for sure, the population of Sesame Street is definitely a wild colony and not a circus or zoo troop. They co-exist with humans, but don't seem to be owned. Rather, they have found little niches, including garbage cans, which they have turned into homes.

Dawn of Cthulhu – Page 192

The phenomenon of transplanted populations is not common, but it's not unheard of. In England, there's a small herd of wild wallabies who are living comfortably in a corner of the English countryside. In New Brunswick, my home province, there was a famous incident where a couple of Japanese Macaques escaped into the wild; they were well adapted to New Brunswick climates, and there was some concern that they might found a breeding colony. There's a long record of Europeans introducing foreign species, usually domesticated or semi-domesticated, which then take off. Horses in North America are an excellent example. Rabbits in Australia are another. Raccoons have turned out to be able colonists in both Japan and Germany.

Indeed, we see colonies of wild but human encultured Mu-Pets in several cities and countries. For instance, colonies have been identified in urban districts in France, Canada, Brazil, Japan and Australia. Some experts suggest that in addition to zoos and circuses, there may be as many as thirty wild colonies, mostly in cities throughout the world.

The Sesame creatures, because of their ability to learn and speak human languages, their non-aggressive ways, and their intelligence are well suited to scavenging at the fringes of human cultures. In a way, they are a lot like other urban invaders, including rats, skunks, pigeons and particularly raccoons. So there's every reason to think that they would be quite successful.

Indeed, they might be more than successful. For their part, the Sesame creatures are friendly, articulate, pose no threats, make few if any demands and generally do not amount to a nuisance. So in this sense, they're actually more adept than even rats, pigeons and raccoons at surviving among humans. Rats are unable to make friendly conversation.

Dawn of Cthulhu – Page 193

The evidence is that the individuals of the Sesame Street colony not only survive among humans, but they're tolerated and actively embraced. There are numerous documented instances of humans on Sesame Street forming friendships with the wild animals, assisting them and protecting them. It appears that there is a long standing tradition, a well established part of the local culture of Sesame Street, to look out for and protect the members of the Mu-Pets colony.

On the other hand, its probably not long term success. The Sesame Street colony, and other identified colonies in other cities are usually quite small. Take both Big Bird and Snuffleupagus. They appear to be sole representatives or at most the products of small family groups. Big Bird might have an aunt and a younger sister, but his parents are absent. Snuffleupagus has parents and a sibling. But in both cases the populations are single family groups.

Clearly, both of these animals are going to have a hard time finding mates. There's a good chance that neither may reproduce, or if they do mate, it will be within their immediate family grouping. There are simply not enough of these animals, absent an external breeding program, to sustain their population. In a generation or two, both the Snuffleupagus and Big Birds of New York might well be extinct.

The situation of Sesame Monsters is a little bit better. Their small size, adaptability, and humanlike features made them far more desirable for pets, zoos and circuses, so larger numbers of them found their way into the human world. Moreover, their assets also allowed them to survive most effectively when reverting to the wild in urban areas. So its not a surprise that the majority of Sesame creatures in urban colonies are Sesame Monsters.

Dawn of Cthulhu – Page 194

But having said that, their situation is not that great. Their populations are small and isolated. While there are enough individuals on Sesame Street to form a borderline viable breeding population, inbreeding is a constant danger, and accidents or disease can cripple a populations reproductive capacity. It's likely that in the long run, the Sesame Street colony, and most urban colonies will fade away.

One solution is to arrange for outbreeding programs, transferring Sesame creatures from other urban colonies, or from Sesame Island to mate with local colonies.

This may be the only hope for the Big Birds of Snuffleupagus in many places. And it may be critical to maintaining the viability and genetic diversity of the Sesame Monsters.

But of course, there are obstacles of various sorts, including jurisdictional problems. One issue for the Sesame Monsters and their allies is that they have so thoroughly embedded in local human culture and language, that this may actually form a barrier to mating.

An English speaking Sesame Monster may simply refuse or be unable to bond and mate a wild specimen from their original home, Sesame Island, or with a French speaking Sesame monster because their mating communication will not synch up.

In any event, by all indications, the Sesame Street colony has been around for a long time. The Sesame Street children's show has been around since1969 and the colony was well established even then. Some of the residents of Sesame Street, such as Mr. Hooper, were quite old even then but were familiar with and comfortable with the creatures. This long and comfortable relationship suggests that the Colony dates back several decades.

Let's hope that the marvelous creatures of the Sesame Street colony will endure for many, many more decades.

A Note from the Author

If you've skipped to the end, looking for an apology, well... Sorry? Also, no refunds!

All kidding aside, I want to thank you for taking the time out to read my little book. If you've made it all the way here, then I'm just going to assume you liked it. And one more thing, I want to ask a favor. If you liked this, could I suggest you leave a review wherever you got it. Mention it to your friends, give it a plug on social media. Say nice things. If that's too much, just toss me a couple of stars.

Writing is a solitary, lonely pursuit and actually getting some feedback or appreciation is a wonderful thing. But there's more to it. It's about trying to get out there. There are a lot of people writing a lot of books, and it can get hard to get noticed. So help a guy out.

So REVIEWS! If you liked this book, or even just some of it, or any other book I've done, go on Goodreads, Reddit, Facebook, any place that hosts reviews and say something nice. It can be long, it can be short, it can be full of nuance and analysis, or just generally kind, it can just be stars or thumbs up. Whatever you want. Spread the word, help people to find it.

In the meantime, check out my website – denvaldron.com

Oh and by the way, I have other books, wonderful books, terrific books. Let me tell you about them…

ALTERNATE REALITIES

A Trilogy or Strange New Worlds

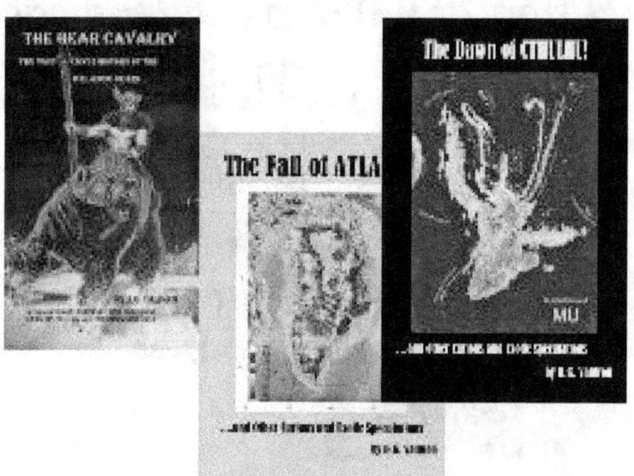

The Fall of Atlantis includes a geo-historical exploration of a real Atlantis ending in a different kind of tragedy; the Retoverse, a fun the accidental cinematic universe of 50s sci fi films, Ancient Rome plausibly crossing the Atlantic, because of coffee(!!!), and the saga of an Alternate Greenland that was never covered by ice.

The Bear Cavalry, the True (Not!) History of the Icelandic Bears, chronicles a history where travelling Vikings domesticated North American Bears and eventually learn to forge them into the most terrifying medieval fight force ever – with excursions into history, biology and art along the way. Bonus story – the Sharebear Apocalypse, is it really just a hug that feels so good.

Dawn of Cthulhu – Page 198

AXIS OF ANDES
NEW WORLD WAR
A History of WWII in South America

Berlin, 1937, Adolph Hitler and his cabinet meet with a strange delegation from Ecuador. The delegates from the small South American nation beg for help, fearing an impending invasion from their rival, Peru. What happens at that meeting sets in motion a chain of events that sets the entire continent on fire. By the time it's done, millions are dead, nations are in ruins, and the map of Latin America will be changed beyond recognition.

FUNNY FANTASY
And COMIC SCIENCE FICTION

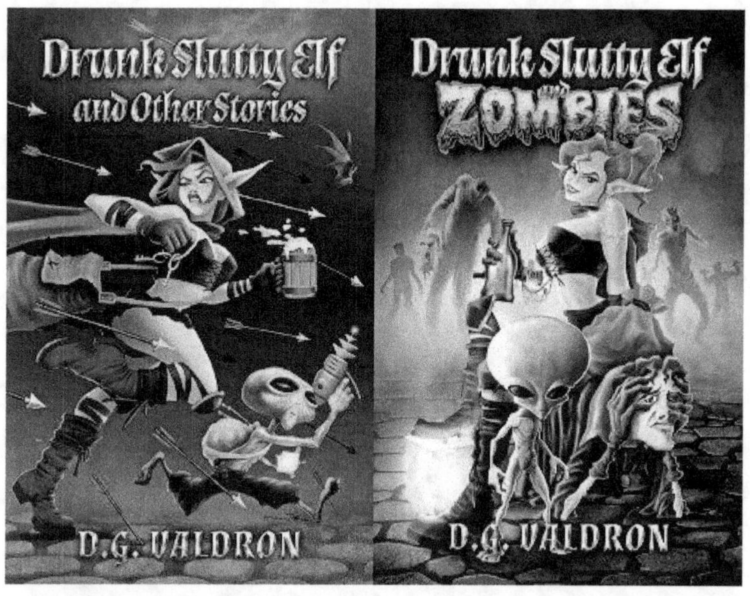

DRUNK SLUTTY ELF AND OTHER STORIES
Plus
DRUNK SLUTTY ELF AND ZOMBIES

Two volumes of savage, satirical, subversive wicked, funny, frantic science fiction and fantasy. Demented ghost hunters, frustrated aliens, horny giants, drunken elves, sneaky ghosts, wayward barbarians and many more.

HEARTS IN DARKNESS

Three Collections of Horror Stories

Featuring riveting stories about a man's cancer learning to talk to him, the ultimate serial killer; Allison, a paralyzed pregnant woman feeling her fetus taking control of her body, a desperate singl mother lured down a dark path; the army enlisting the unkillable men in the masks; Silence about a thief hiding in the home of a killer; a ghost that haunts the people around its victim, and many, many more. Melancholy darkness, chilling horror, dark visions.

The Pirates Histories of Doctor Who

The greatest, most professional Doctor Who fan films ever made, explorations of the peculiarities of copyright, the developments of new technologies, the evolution of fan culture, and histories of the Doctor on stage, in audio, and in animation. These books are full of new and entertaining insights and revelations that you'll love.

LEXX UNAUTHORIZED

LEXX a show about a giant space bug that blows up planets, the cowardly security guard who is its captain, and the undead assassin, runaway love slave, and robot head who form its crew.

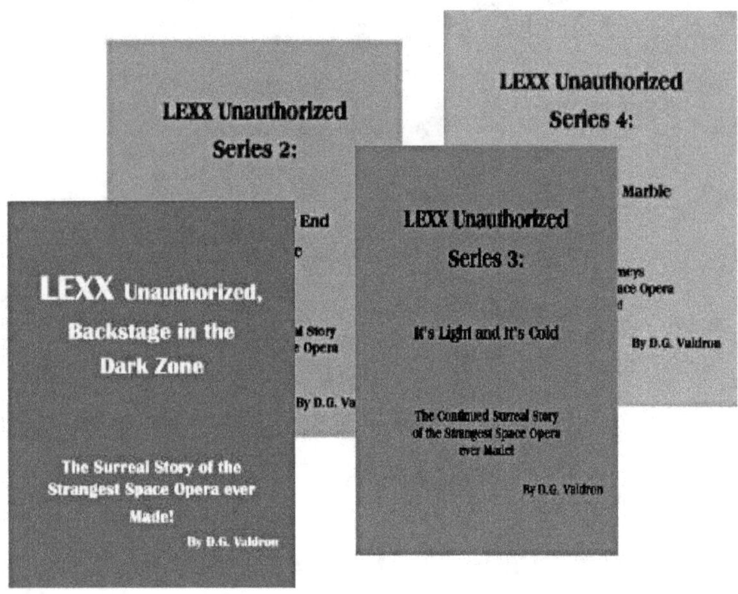

Originally billed as 'Star Trek's Evil Twin,' the cultiest of cult sci fi, LEXX's forte was black humor, startling visuals, big ideas, and a sensibility that had more to do with surrealists like Jodorowsky or Bunuel than mainstream science fiction. And, as unconventional as it was onscreen, the story of how it came to be is even more bizarre.

A Dark Fantasy
of Murder and Redemption

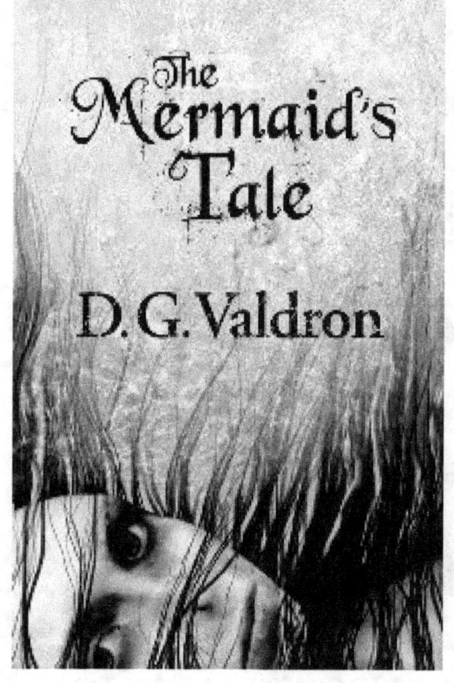

There's a City where all the races come together uneasily.

There's a Civil War gathering, and dark powers assembling.

There's a Mermaid, murdered cruelly, her people distraught.

There's an Orc, lowest and the worst, assigned to solve the murder, before it all comes crashing down.

And there's something else: this world's first serial killer.

Dawn of Cthulhu – Page 204

STARLOST UNAUTHORIZED

And the Quest for Canadian Identity

The series that was Harlan Ellison's nemesis. The most controversial series in the history of sci fi television. This exhaustively researched book, based on interviews with some of the stars and writers, brings a fresh new interpretation of of the Starlost, and a re-evaluation of the series and its themes in the context of the 1970s crisis of Canadian nationalism.

Dawn of Cthulhu – Page 205

TWILIGHT OF ECHELON

Published by

AT BAY PRESS

Based on the work of famed artist Robert Pasternak the book features paintings from Pasternak's Echelon series, accompanied by stories written independently by D.G. Valdron, Lovern Kindzierski, Alex Passey and Blaise Moritz

Dawn of Cthulhu – Page 206